'I *was* a pirate. Now I'm trying to give it up, and I need help.'

Uncle Ludovic has a great black beard hanging down his chest like a doormat. He claims to be a pirate trying to mend his ways.

One summer Caroline and Nicholas spend a wonderful holiday with him — there's breakfast on the beach, swimming and sailing, and treasure hunting in the house when it rains.

Sometimes Uncle Ludovic certainly does some very piratical things. But soon Caroline hits on a sure way to reform their pirate uncle.

An intriguing tale which boys and girls of a wide age range will enjoy.

MARGARET MAHY

The Pirate Uncle

Illustrated by Mary Dinsdale

Puffin Books

Puffin Books

Penguin Books (N.Z.) Ltd, 182–190 Wairau Road,
Auckland 10, New Zealand
Penguin Books Ltd, Harmondsworth,
Middlesex, England
Penguin Books, 40 West 23rd Street,
New York, N.Y. 10010, U.S.A.
Penguin Books Australia Ltd, Ringwood,
Victoria, Australia
Penguin Books Canada Limited, 2801 John Street,
Markham, Ontario, Canada L3R 1B4

First published by J. M. Dent and Sons 1974
Published in Puffin Books 1987
Reprinted 1987

Printed in Hong Kong

Contents

Contents

1. Two Children are Sent to Stay with a Mysterious Uncle

Nicholas Battle, nine years old, thin, fair and thoughtful, was sitting behind the chair in the corner of the sitting-room reading a really good book. It was about two children who had been sent to stay with a mysterious uncle who lived in Cornwall, England. (A lot of good stories begin like this.) Nick hadn't got very far in the story yet, but already he was pretty sure that the uncle was a smuggler and possibly a highwayman too. What he did not know was that a coincidence was about to happen.

Into the room came Nick's mother Gillian Battle and his father Andy Battle having one of their private discussions that was half a joke and half an argument. Of course they did not know that Nick was concealed behind the chair in his secret-reading space.

"I'd love to go," Nick's mother was saying, "but what about the kids?"

"It's school holidays!" Andy Battle replied in his gay off-hand way. "Someone could look after them for us."

"Who?" cried Gillian Battle. "Just who?" She sat down in an armchair.

"What about your mother? She's fond of them."

"Being fond of them doesn't necessarily mean you want them living with you in a small flat for two weeks," was the reply. "I wouldn't dream of leaving them with her. She's not as young as she used to be, and they can be a handful at times."

"Oh, for goodness sake, Gilly," — in a voice, laughing and impatient at the same time — "they're a couple of lambs. In fact, if anything, they're a bit *too* lamb-like. They sometimes worry me they're so quiet and obedient. Too much lamb and not enough lion."

Before Nicholas had time to feel indignant at being called "too lamb-like", his mother was indignant for him.

"They're perfectly normal, lively children, Andy Battle!" she cried, and there was no doubt that there was quite a lot of the lion about *her* when it came to sticking up for her children. "I wouldn't enjoy myself if I thought they were being a trouble to anyone."

"Well, there's only one thing for it," Andy Battle said firmly, "they'll have to stay with old Ludovic."

Behind the chair Nick sat up taller in surprise. Ludovic was his father's brother. Nick had always wondered why his mother was suspicious of him.

"That pirate!" she exclaimed indignantly. "I

wouldn't trust him with a couple of hedgehogs, let alone two children."

"Now Gilly, don't forget . . . " Andy Battle argued back, "he was like a father to me, when our own dad died, and look how good and respectable I am. I wear a tie, cut my hair and shine my shoes. I cut the lawn and weed the garden. I've even given up smoking. I'm a model husband and father, and handsome too."

"Yes, well . . . " said Gillian Battle, giggling a bit, "don't forget it isn't your tatty old brother Ludovic who's made you like that. It's me! You were a sort of ocean-going hippie when I married you. Now you've got a good job, you're clean, and I can take you anywhere. If Ludovic had *his* way you'd still be wild, like a field of thistles."

"All the same," said Andy Battle, "it wouldn't do the kids any harm to be thistly for a bit, and as I've got to go to Sydney and I'd like to take you with me, and you don't want the kids to be a trouble to anyone, Ludovic's the answer."

"Hm!" she said, not convinced. She got up. "I must go and put the dinner on. But let me tell you, Andy Battle, everyone — even Mrs Donald — says they're the best-behaved children in the street, and what's more . . . " But as she said this she marched out of the room with Andy Battle following, and the door was closed after them. Nick could hear them in the kitchen, laughing and arguing, turn and turn about.

Nick stood up cautiously and came out from behind his chair. Then he did something forbidden.

He stood on one of the good chairs with his shoes on so that he could peer at himself in the looking-glass. Eyes, two, green — ears, two, pink — nose, one — mouth, one — hair, short and hay-coloured . . . ordinary enough, thought Nick, not too polite, not too wild! What would it be like to be thistly? Nick practised a smile trying to see himself as his father saw him. His reflection smiled back in a careful way, not letting itself be caught out.

"Hello," said a voice behind him. "What are you smiling at?" It was Nick's sister Caroline, small and pretty, with blue eyes, not green ones, and the same hay-coloured hair in plaits tied with pink ribbons.

Nick could not explain that he was watching his own smile. He tried to surprise her with news instead.

"Hey, we might be going away for a holiday," he hissed.

Caroline blinked as if he had suddenly started to speak some unknown outer-space language.

"You're standing on a chair with shoes on," she said at last. Nick thought that this was like Caroline, and that it was all her fault if people said they were the best-behaved children in the street.

"A holiday . . ." he repeated, ". . . without Mum and Dad. We might be going to stay with——"

But at this very moment Mr and Mrs Battle came back into the room, hand in hand, and Andy Battle spoke out in the triumphant voice of one who has won a great victory. "Just the kids we wanted to see," he cried. "We've got some great news for you. You'll never guess what your great little mother has worked out for us all . . . "

12

Caroline was about to be astonished by the great news, but Nick already knew what it was. He and Caroline were going to learn how to be thistly in a pirate's house, and Nick did not know whether to be pleased or sorry.

2. Meeting Uncle Ludovic

When you have been reading a book about two children staying with an uncle who is a smuggler and suddenly you find you are being sent to stay with an uncle who might be a pirate, it is rather like being haunted. Nick felt nervous about reading the next chapter in his book because of what might be revealed. Anyhow, things were very rushed for a while and he did not have much chance to go on with his book. The phoning, the packing, the kissing and hugging, the waving goodbye. . . . All these things were over at last and Nick and Caroline found themselves on a bus driving off into the world, not having any clear idea of the day ahead. It had become a jungle of unexpectedness, instead of the clear pleasant path they were used to.

"How will we know Uncle Ludovic?" Nick had

asked. "We don't want to go home with just any stranger who might be a kidnapper perhaps."

Nick had been joking but Caroline looked alarmed.

"Look for a perambulating haystack with bare feet," his mother had said grimly. "That will certainly be your Uncle Ludovic."

"Don't you like him?" Caroline had asked her nervously.

Mrs Battle had laughed suddenly. "Oh yes, I like him a lot, but we'd never agree if we had to stay under the same roof. We're better liking each other from a distance."

Their mother was quite light-hearted about it all, once she had made up her mind.

Nicholas tried to read his book on the bus though it made his head ache. He thought he might get some clue about what was going to happen.

In the book it was January with a white snow storm coming down around the dark house. It was January with Nicholas and Caroline too, but there was no snow to be seen through the window of the bus, not even on the tops of the mountains. Instead January had breathed like a dragon on the land, burning the paddocks brown and gold. The nor-west wind made the trees bow and sway before the bus, and lifted the dust from the dry paddocks into the air.

"Quite different!" Nicholas thought, though it worried him that it should be January in the book and in the bus too.

When the bus stopped, it was in the middle of nowhere. "O.K. you kids — get off here," said the

16

driver, and he swung himself down from the bus to get their suitcases from the luggage compartment at the back.

Like nervous explorers testing the water of strange seas, Nicholas and Caroline got off too.

They saw the uncle at once. He was the only person there, but even if they had been meeting him at some crowded airport they would have noticed him immediately. He had a beard hanging down on his chest like a black doormat. Not only this, his hair was long and he had a moustache. Neither Nicholas nor Caroline had ever expected to be related to such a hairy person. He wore blue jeans, a sloppy shirt and Roman sandals.

"How do you do?" said the uncle. "Nicholas and Caroline is it?"

"Uncle Ludovic, I presume," Nicholas said, thinking of the famous African explorers, Stanley and Livingstone, and then he blushed because his voice sounded so pompous.

The uncle shook hands with them both at the same time which meant that Caroline had to make do with his left hand — not good manners. Then he scooped up their suitcases and started to carry them off. Caroline and Nicholas had to scuttle to keep up with him. Though he was short for an uncle — shorter than their father anyway — he took long steps and moved like a person who was used to a lot of space around him.

He put their suitcases on the roof rack of a rather battered and grubby mini that was parked by the roadside. He was quiet as he did this, thinking about what to say next. Nicholas and Caroline thought too. All Nicholas could think of were the words "perambulating haystack", and all Caroline could think of was asking him why he did not clean his car. The uncle opened the door for them and they got in in silence. Never before had they been in such an untidy car. The blue carpeting that covered the floor had sand and shells on it. The glove box was open. Caroline knew just what was in the glove box of her mother's car . . . a pair of gloves, a ball-point pen and a note book in which her mother wrote down how much petrol she bought and how many miles the car went before she had to buy some more. Uncle Ludovic had one glove in his glove box, but as well as that he had a small book called *Neutrons. . . particles of the future. . .* some maps held together with a bulldog paper clip, a cellophane bag of peppermints, a detective story, some orange peel and a screw driver. Sitting in the back Nicholas found he was sharing it with a coil of rope and several wooden things that he did not recognize.

Nobody could think of anything to say. It began to look as if nobody would say anything for the next two weeks. Then Caroline gave a sudden squeak.

"What is it?" asked Uncle Ludovic anxiously.

"There's a spider in its web," Caroline said.

"Oh yes," said Uncle Ludovic "That's *Theriodon veruculatum.*"

"*Theri* — what?" asked Nicholas, liking the sound of the long words.

"It's a tangle-web spider," Uncle Ludovic said. "I don't know what it is doing here. They often live on

18

gorse bushes. Perhaps it thought my car was a gorse bush. I'll put *Theriodon veruculatum* off on the next real gorse bush we come to."

"You could squash it," said Caroline, looking at *Theriodon veruculatum* with dislike.

"Oh no!" said Uncle Ludovic. "I like her too much. Her web looks untidy but it's actually better planned than it looks, and she's got a nice yellow patch on her."

"She should know better than to get into cars," said Caroline severely.

They were coming to some hills and the car was beginning to go slowly. Nobody said anything for a few minutes.

"It was clever of you to recognize me," the uncle said at last.

"There was only you, so we thought it must be you," Caroline replied. "I didn't know you had such a big beard though."

"Ah," said the uncle deeply. "You noticed it then, did you?"

"We weren't staring," Nicholas said from the back seat, in case Uncle Ludovic suspected rudeness. "We couldn't help seeing it."

Uncle Ludovic stroked his beard with one hand, and somewhere in the tangle of beard and moustache they saw his teeth as he grinned.

The road got steeper and steeper, winding up through brown tussocky hills. Streaks of bush grew in the creases and gullies, but mostly the hills were bare. Nicholas thought that it was like driving over the vast hairy flank of some sleeping brown creature. He thought that the hills might suddenly twitch and throw them off back down to the plains below.

They came to the top of the hill unexpectedly and looked down on the other side at a soft green sea, freckled with boats. The arms of the land curled around it in a kindly fashion and almost met . . . almost but not quite. There was a small break between the headlands where the sea of the bay and the sea of the great ocean beyond, flowed into each other.

"There it is," said Uncle Ludovic proudly. "The snuggest little bay on the coast." He pulled into the side of the road, and looked seriously at Caroline and a little less seriously at Nicholas. "Now I'm going to tell you something . . . something so terribly secret and secretly terrible I'd only trust really close relations. Do you know why you're here?"

"To have a holiday," said Caroline.

"So that Mum and Dad can have a break from us," said Nicholas.

"Both wrong!" the uncle cried. "That was just a trick, a ruse, to get you here. The fact is, I need your help."

Nicholas and Caroline stared at him, wondering how on earth they could be expected to help an uncle they had only just met.

"Are you listening?" he asked. "Well then, I'll begin. Has your mother ever called me a pirate? I'll bet she has, and she is right. I'm not just an uncle. I am a pirate too. It's the pirate part of me that grows the whiskers."

"A pirate!" Nicholas repeated, thinking it sounded almost too remarkable to say aloud.

"Yes, a pirate . . . or rather I *was* a pirate. Now I'm trying to give it up and I need help. That's why I sent for you."

"To be a sort of Pirates Anonymous?" Nicholas asked, grinning.

Uncle Ludovic did not grin back. He nodded seriously. "I want you to help me reform. I need good characters around me — people of the highest moral standards to remind me to behave."

"We're good," Caroline cried smugly. "People say we're the best children in the street."

"We haven't had much practice with pirates though," Nicholas said in his thoughtful way. "There aren't many of them around. How did you come to take up being a pirate, Uncle Ludovic?"

Uncle Ludovic's face bunched up under his beard. He was smiling. "I see I shall have to Tell You All," he said, trying to sound regretful. He looked at the sea and sighed deeply.

3. A Pirate's Dilemma

"I was always a wild lad," Uncle Ludovic said reflectively, ". . . never happy to settle down with my feet under a table. I ran away from home you know."

"How did you run away?" asked Caroline.

"Pretty fast for the first two hundred yards and then slower after that," Uncle Ludovic replied. "And at last I was walking. I walked away from home to the sea. I think I always had a bit of salt in me that the sea called to, you know. Some people are sour some are sweet and I was salty — that's how it was."

"Did you start being a pirate straight away?" Caroline asked sternly.

"Bit by bit really," Uncle Ludovic said. "It crept up on me as it were. First I started wearing pirate boots and then I won a sword playing cards. Well, there's no point in having a sword and not wearing it is there?"

"You could hang it on the wall," Nicholas suggested, but Uncle Ludovic shook his head.

"No good doing that on a ship," he said sadly, "it just keeps falling off again. No, you've got to wear a sword if you've got one, or it's a wicked waste. And once you've got a sword at your side, well, it makes you *think* pirate if you know what I mean. And then other pirates began to recognize me. I was led astray by jolly companions. And then I got treasure fever."

"Treasure fever?" asked Nicholas doubtfully.

"A sickness pirates get. They just have to find treasure. I looked for it everywhere. Dived for it in deep seas, dug over whole islands."

"Did you find any?" Caroline asked intently.

"Oh yes, we were always finding it. Gold, you know! Jewels, pearls, and that sort of thing."

"You must have got very rich," Caroline remarked.

"Not *very* rich," Uncle Ludovic mumbled sadly. "I spent it on riotous living you know. And then we priates would fight over it night and day. I lost a lot through fighting. And then there's income tax and other land-lubberly expenses. One way and another I've lost a lot of treasure in my time."

Caroline asked, "Did you ever drink rum, Uncle, when you were a pirate?"

"No, no never." Uncle Ludovic shook his head so that his beard swept busily over his wide chest. Then he looked at Caroline sideways. "Well, sometimes perhaps — just a little. A mere drop! Quite a lot at times! Being a pirate without tossing down rum is like

24

being a vulture and turning down a nice meal of dead camel. No one has faith in a pirate who doesn't drink rum."

"And you want us to help you reform?" Nicholas asked in an expressionless voice. He was trying not to sound suspicious. It was all very well for Caroline to believe Uncle Ludovic was a pirate. She had half believed it to begin with. It was easy for her to believe the other half. It was not quite so easy for Nicholas. Yet Uncle Ludovic did not seem to be altogether joking. It was as if he was seeing it all so clearly — himself as a gay adventurous young man easily led astray by jolly companions and a sword that just had to be used.

"The trouble is," he said now in a worried voice, "it's got to be such a habit with me. I find myself burying treasure, any old treasure, and singing wicked pirate songs, attacking any ships I can get at. It's really pathetic. You'd weep to see it. And suppose I went into good society and met some duchess dripping with diamonds, why I'd out with my cutlass and with a hoarse cry I'd . . ."

"There aren't any duchesses in New Zealand," Caroline interrupted.

"Every one's equal, except that some people are richer."

"Suppose he met the Mayor, though," Nicholas said, becoming interested against his better judgement. "The Mayor wears a gold chain."

"There you are," Uncle Ludovic went on, giving Nicholas a grateful look. "I can just see myself being introduced to the Mayor. Suddenly my eyes fall on his golden chain and it brings out the worst in me. My hand twitches, and before I can prevent it I've drawn my trusty cutlass. The Mayor is holding out his hand to greet me, but I slash at him and try to snatch his chain and mayoral jewels. You know what that would mean! Social disgrace and ignominy. I need help to break such habits before I set sail among the best people. Do you think you could help me?"

"You don't *have* to wear a cutlass, of course," Nicholas said. "You could leave it at home."

Uncle Ludovic looked at him gratefully. "A good suggestion straight off," he cried. "I knew you'd help me. By the time I've been in your company a couple of weeks I'll be able to go anywhere among the best people without any criticism or comment."

"But you're supposed to be looking after us," Caroline pointed out. "Grown-ups should look after children, not the other way round."

"That doesn't count with pirates," Uncle Ludovic said emphatically. "Pirates don't come under that rule. Uncles do but pirates don't. It's all part of the dilemma."

"The dilemma?" asked Caroline, wrinkling her nose at the strange word.

"Being half uncle and half pirate *is* a dilemma," Uncle Ludovic said frankly. He started the car again saying cheerfully, "But you're going to be such a help. I've only just met you but I feel I've known you both for years."

Caroline looked at Nicholas and saw he was grinning, so she grinned too, rather uncertainly, staring at Uncle Ludovic as if he might begin some

26

piratical behaviour at any moment.

The road wound down and down.

At last Uncle Ludovic turned the car to the left, down a little lane overgrown with periwinkles and rambling scrambling roses and a moment later turned right into an open garage. It was shadowy in this garage after the bright day outside, but Nicholas could see that it was crowded with many things . . . garden tools, boxes and a lot of bits and pieces of machinery. Up above his head he saw dim shapes slung against the rafters.

"They look like boats," he thought. "Real boats!" But before he could make out the shapes properly he found himself marching down a path following Caroline, who was following Uncle Ludovic, who was carrying the cases.

An unexpected shape, brown and shaggy, suddenly joined in their marching. At first Nicholas thought it was a dog, but a moment later, after blinking, he saw it was a sheep. Caroline exclaimed with some alarm. The sheep, though woolly, was large and jostling.

"That's Bunty," Uncle Ludovic said. "You may think a sheep is a funny pet for a pirate, but we've got a lot in common really. My mother died when I was young and so did Bunty's. I think Bunty thinks that I'm her mother, and in a way I am, because I brought her up from lambhood on bottles of milk."

"Maybe your beard reminds her of her mother," Caroline said seriously. "I think you both look rather woolly."

They went on down the path in Indian file between

bushy shrubs and tall silver birches, pebbles and shells appeared underfoot and patches of alyssum and virginian stock grew among the ferns and feathery grass on either side. The path twisted and widened and there was the uncle's house. Looking at that house Nicholas could well believe Uncle Ludovic was really a pirate. It was more like a bird's nest than a house for it was overgrown with ivy and other sprawling vines. Through the leaves windows framed in red looked at them. It all had a nautical air as if built by a ship's carpenter on a desert island. The red door was slightly open like a surprised mouth. The uncle pushed through it. Bunty went after him, Caroline went in after Bunty and Nicholas after Caroline.

The house was lined with panels of wood, smoothed and polished to a soft honey colour. It was like being in a room with walls of gold. There was a fireplace piled with cones, a shining brass coal bucket, a bookcase bulging with books, a ship in a bottle, a coil of rope in one corner and a jamjar of ferns on the table.

"Your room is here," Uncle Ludovic said, and showed them into a little room, hardly bigger than a cupboard. There were hooks and coat hangers on the back of the door and two bunks against the wall opposite the door, tucked in with tartan rugs and with a sheepskin at the foot of each.

"You hang your clothes on the back of the door," Uncle Ludovic said. "Anything you don't need to hang up you can leave in your cases and push under the bottom bunk. No messing things up! Everything shipshape!"

29

"We don't mess things," Caroline said indignantly, but she and Nicholas looked at the bunks lovingly. They had never slept in bunks before. Nicholas felt a funny warm feeling as if this tiny room and its bunks were the first real proof he had had, that he was going to enjoy his holiday.

It took them only a short time to unpack and go back into the first room. Uncle Ludovic had unfolded a table from the wall and had set it with a cherry cake and a cold roast chicken.

"It seems like a special lunch," Caroline said rather impressed.

"Not really!" Uncle Ludovic answered. "Pirates are always eating chicken and cherry cake, cherry cake and chicken." Bunty who had been put outside looked in at the door and bleated.

"All right," Uncle Ludovic said. "You can have a slice in a minute, Bunty. I've spoiled that sheep," he went on. "She thinks she should have cherry cake too. Now sit down and eat. . . no knives and forks because it's a fingers lunch. There are some paper napkins, so you don't have to wipe your fingers on your clothes. Pirates wipe their fingers on their beards but I'm trying to give up being a pirate as you may remember, so I'm going in for politeness. And you two haven't got beards anyway . . . not yet."

4. Pirate Trouble

That afternoon there was the first pirate trouble of the holiday. Lunch was over, fingers were washed and the cake was shut in its tin.

"Now to show you around," Uncle Ludovic said. "I really love the place I live in so I shall enjoy showing you."

He led them across his tiny lawn and down a thin, twisting path onto the beach. It was a little curved new moon of sand and sea between two rocky headlands, looking almost empty of people except for a red roof poking out of the bush high on the eastern ridge. Cutting into the sea was a small jetty and beside the jetty, light as a leaf on the water, was a boat.

"Is it yours?" asked Nicholas getting an excited look in his eyes.

"My very own," said Uncle Ludovic in a boastful

voice. "It's got a Stewart engine and a woodstove in the cabin and I can go anywhere on the bay in her. It cost me a fortune, that engine did, but it's been worth every penny,"

"There's a baby boat too!" cried Caroline. "Look Nick — the boat's got a baby."

"That's a dinghy," said Nicholas. "That *is* a dinghy, isn't it?"

"It is," replied Uncle Ludovic. "Both my boats are called *Sinbad* . . . big *Sinbad* and little *Sinbad*. Do you see the eyes painted up by the bows? That's so's the *Sinbads* can see which way to go, even in the dark."

Sure enough, each boat had a merry eye, painted in white, staring out over the sea. Nicholas and Caroline gazed at the *Sinbads* very respectfully. Then a movement out by one of the headlands caught Caroline's eye.

"Uncle Ludovic, you've got a visitor."

The uncle stared. A man in a blue canoe had come around the headland and was paddling peacefully towards the jetty. He was young-looking and wore a coloured summer shirt.

"Out upon it!" muttered Uncle Ludovic. He made his shoulders look broader and his beard more bristly. "Some marauding son of a sea cook! I feel a bit piratish. I must strike the lubber down."

Before the children could do a thing, their uncle had raced along the beach and down the jetty. He seized a yard broom which was leaning against the rail.

"He looks more like a witch than a pirate," Nicholas said. His eyebrows looked puzzled, but his mouth was smiling at the edges. Uncle Ludovic scrambled down the jetty steps and into the smaller *Sinbad*.

He sent little *Sinbad* out over the water with a single oar — more of a short paddle, really — worked over the stern of the boat with a curious wriggle.

"I thought you had to have paddles on both sides," Caroline said. She and Nicholas were both following the uncle's footsteps down the jetty.

"I thought so too," Nicholas agreed. "He's taken the broom. Perhaps he's going to row with that." But he didn't really think so.

"Avast there!" they heard Uncle Ludovic shout. "Avast there, scum!"

"You see . . . he really *is* a pirate," Caroline said in an excited voice. "That's a thing pirates say. He's using pirate words."

"The man in the canoe doesn't seem very worried," said Nicholas doubtfully. Caroline shook her head. "He wouldn't expect to find a pirate," she pointed out. "It will be a terrible shock to him."

The canoe man had stopped paddling and was watching the little boat approach. They heard the sound of his voice which was low and pleasant, but not the words he was saying. However nothing the man said made any difference to Uncle Ludovic who was carried away by a piratical frenzy. It was impossible for a man in a mere canoe wearing a mere summer shirt to placate a furious uncle with a bristling beard. The uncle stopped rowing and seized the broom from the bottom of little *Sinbad*. He leaped to his feet and began sweeping at the stranger, balancing himself in the rocking boat with tremendous skill. Now it was the stranger's turn to start shouting.

"Stop it, stop it you mad fool, you'll have me over."

"Prepare to receive boarders!" yelled Uncle Ludovic, as little *Sinbad* nudged the canoe. Both boats rocked sharply. Caroline screamed with excitement, just as she would have at a film. As for Nicholas . . . he was astounded. Could that pirate story be even slightly true after all?

"Prepare to receive boarders, you lily-livered land-lubber!" shouted Uncle Ludovic again, and pushed at the summer shirt with his broom. The canoe and little *Sinbad* shot apart again. The summer shirt tried to hit Uncle Ludovic with his paddle, but it was too long to handle easily. Goaded beyond all common sense, the summer shirt tried to stand up. Now he was at Uncle Ludovic's mercy. With a cry of triumph Uncle Ludovic lunged with his broom, the canoe rocked wildly and the summer shirt fell into the water.

He fell quite slowly, waving his arms and legs as he went. He looked like a paper windmill, bright and spinning, falling to a watery doom.

"He's gone, he's gone!" Caroline yelled, horrified to find she was laughing at some strange grown-up falling into the water, but laughing all the same in an astonished fashion.

"And there goes Uncle!" Nicholas answered.

Sure enough, flinging his arms wide and giving a terrible yell, Uncle Ludovic fell face forward into the sea. The green water swallowed them eagerly.

Little *Sinbad,* the blue canoe, the paddle and the broom were left bobbling anxiously on the ripples.

"Sunk forever," cried Caroline dramatically. "Sharks will get them — oh no, there they are!" she added, as first the summer shirt, and then Uncle Ludovic bobbed up again, and then stood up streaming with water.

After all the sea was not much deeper than their waists. It occurred to Nicholas that there was something splendid about seeing two people standing, fully dressed, waist-deep in water.

"They're crying," said Caroline suddenly. "Have they got cramp?"

"They're laughing," Nicholas answered.

"I almost laughed," Caroline replied, smoothing her face carefully. "I would have laughed if it had been a film. Look, Nick — they're bringing their boats in to the beach."

They ran back down the jetty and onto the sand to meet the summer shirt and Uncle Ludovic.

Nicholas had the feeling that Uncle Ludovic hadn't finished yet . . .

He was right about this. When Uncle Ludovic had dragged the little *Sinbad* into the shallow water he suddenly let go and sat down in the water again, his face in his hands. He was so wet it did not matter any more from the point of view of more wetness, but it looked remarkable to see a person sit down in the water when the sand was only a few feet away. He sobbed loudly.

"What have I done?" he cried. "What have I done? I've blotted my escutcheon. All my good resolutions gone, like snow upon the desert's dusty face."

Nicholas was taking off his shoes and socks. As he waded out to his uncle, his feet looked like ghostly fish sliding along under the water.

"But what chance did I have?" Uncle Ludovic went on, obviously enjoying himself very much indeed. "Orphaned at an early age, at a mere twenty-two years, cast upon the wicked world . . . ah, dear sir, forgive me. Don't bring my grey hairs in sorrow to the grave."

"There, there!" said the summer shirt. "Of course I won't." He was pulling his canoe up onto the sand.

"He's trying to reform," Caroline explained to him hastily. "He wants to give up his wild life and go into good society with rich people."

"I'd say he had his work well and truly cut out, then," the summer shirt replied.

"We're helping him," Caroline boasted proudly.

Nicholas was taking no notice of all this. He laid his hand firmly on little *Sinbad* and started pulling her in. He felt a peculiar magic flow out of the sunwarmed wood tingling like electricity in his wrists. She followed him obediently, trusting his guiding hands.

Caroline went on explaining earnestly to the summer shirt, believing the uncle's story because she liked it and wanted to believe it. "He's trying to give up being a pirate, but he slips back from time to time. It's one of his habits to upset boats," she declared as if she had known about such things for years. Uncle Ludovic wept noisily and the summer-shirt man patted his shoulder.

"I won't be hard on you," the summer-shirt man

promised. "I think every pirate should be given a chance to make good. But perhaps you could think of some way to make up for the wickedness you have done."

"A cup of tea?" suggested Uncle Ludovic.

"And a change of clothes," said the wet stranger rubbing his hands over his wet shirt, wilted like a summer flower.

"An old sea dog's blessing on you," Uncle Ludovic cried, leaping to his feet and shaking himself like a real sea dog.

Slowly they wound a wet way up the bush path.

"And what's your name, Mister?" asked Uncle Ludovic as they went.

"David Carter," replied the summer shirt. He was a youngish man with bright blue eyes and rather longish fair hair.

"Oh, I've heard of you," Uncle Ludovic said thoughtfully. "Aren't you something in the religious line?"

"I'm the Anglican minister for the area," David Carter answered. "But you remind me of someone. Can we have met before?"

"Have you ever been a pirate?" asked Uncle Ludovic.

"Uncle Ludovic, a minister wouldn't be a pirate," Caroline declared, alarmed now at the thought of her uncle sweeping a Reverend into the sea.

"You don't look like a minister," Nicholas said rather shyly. "A pirate could mistake you quite easily for an ordinary victim."

"True," said David Carter. "I must admit I didn't

expect things to be quite so colourful but I might get some idea for a sermon out of it . . . something about forgiving any enemies who sweep you out of your canoe with a broom."

"It sounds a powerful theme," Uncle Ludovic said. "It might be a move in the right direction if we all come to hear it."

The tea was made while David Carter changed into some dry clothes. Uncle Ludovic's blue jeans were rather short for him but he did not complain. The cherry cake was taken out of its tin and some new biscuits appeared — the sort that are joined together with jam and sprinkled with pink sugar. Bunty looked through the door at them and stole Caroline's piece of cake when she wasn't looking. Not that it mattered. There was plenty for another large slice. And after this David Carter set off back to the beach and his blue canoe carrying his wet clothes wrapped in a towel. He shook hands with Caroline and Nicholas and said to Caroline, "Watch that uncle of yours. I think he likes showing off too much. He's going to need constant watching."

"We'll watch him," Caroline replied with great confidence.

"He'll probably improve quite quickly from now on. Be careful he doesn't turn you into a pirate girl," David Carter said with a smile and a wave as he vanished down the path to the beach.

Later that evening the moon, almost full, looked in through the leaves around the open window and saw Nicholas and Caroline tucked up in their bunks.

"It seems a long way from home," Caroline said with a little sigh. "I wonder if Mummy and Dad are all right."

"Of course they are," Nicholas assured her.

"I feel I've known Uncle Ludovic for years and years," Caroline went on. "I didn't think he'd be such a good cook did you?" She hesitated and then asked, "Hey Nick, do you think the uncle *knew* David Carter before he swept him out of the canoe today?"

Nicholas smiled in the black and silver night. "They must be friends," he replied drowsily. "David Carter knew where to find the cherry cake when we were setting the tea. He knew just where the tin was."

Caroline thought about this for a moment. Then she turned over in her bunk. "Good night, Nick," she said.

"Goodnight, Caroline."

5. An Unexpected Breakfast

Nicholas woke early.
He knew it was early because the sunlight on the wall had a rich golden look and not the white clear look it got later in the day. Besides it felt early. There was a sort of early stillness about everything — an early softness in the air. Outside he knew the sky was already blue, the day was ripening like an apple. It was going to be hot.

A moment later Nick wondered how he thought of the morning as silent. In fact it was full of singing birds, but he had not heard them all at once. His ears had been reaching out beyond them. Now he could hear their voices embroidering the stillness with threads of sound. Then he began to hear other sounds . . . Caroline breathing — snoring slightly in the bunk below him and, outside — almost like part

41

of the silence — the big sighing breath that was the sea washing in on the sand.

Nicholas did not get up straight away. He had a few thinking moments and he set out to use them by thinking.

He thought of the mysterious way his life was following his book and felt under his pillow to see if his book was there safely. He thought of his mysterious uncle who could almost be a pirate attacking the vicar and pushing him into the water. And that made him think of Caroline. It seemed to Nicholas that Caroline was behaving in an unexpected fashion. She was enjoying the pirate uncle just as if she was a sort of pirate herself and not the best behaved girl in the street at home. It puzzled Nicholas. He himself was amused and suspicious, waiting to see what would happen next, like when he read his book, but Caroline had made herself a part of the story and had settled down as if she had been in it from the very beginning.

Nicholas sighed and began reading. It grew more exciting and more exciting still. The children in the story woke one morning to find their smuggler uncle had vanished: the snow lay deep around the house of mystery. No footsteps could be seen coming or going but the smuggler uncle had disappeared entirely. Nick's mouth hung open a little bit as he read and the patches of sunlight moved over the wall as the sun outside rose higher.

"Nick!" said Caroline sharply.

She was one of those sudden wakers who don't want to read or think first thing in the morning.

Nicholas sighed and leaned over the edge of the bunk.

"Hello," he said.

"Gosh, you look funny upside down," Caroline remarked. "I've never seen you upside down before."

"Sorry!" said Nick sarcastically.

"That's all right," Caroline replied earnestly. "You look better upside down. If I was you I'd always walk on my hands."

Nick thought about hitting her for cheekiness but it was too far to reach down.

"Shall we get up and see what Uncle Ludovic is doing?" he asked.

"He'll be asleep dreaming of treasure," Caroline cried leaping out of bed. "His hand will be twitching for his bloody sword — that's not swearing," she put in quickly. "I mean a sword with blood on it. You're allowed to say it if it's about something with blood on it."

When they were dressed, Nick in his brown shorts and yellow T. shirt, Caroline in her pink gingham frock, they went out into the honey coloured living-room. It was very tidy, very clean, very still, very empty.

"Uncle!" Called Caroline. "Uncle — we're up." But there was no answer.

There were two other doors out of the living-room: one to the kitchen and one to the uncle's bedroom. Both doors were open. Nicholas and Caroline could see the uncle's bed made and tucked in. He was not asleep. The kitchen was empty. He was not cooking breakfast.

"He has disappeared," said Caroline.

Nicholas said, "In my book the uncle has gone missing too."

"It's nothing to do with your book," Caroline said firmly. "He's just gone to get the milk or something. But then her eye fell on a sheet of paper on the table. "He's left us a message," she cried. "No — no it isn't, it's a picture of some flags and then some writing."

"Ships send messages by flags," Nicholas told her, looking over her shoulder.

"Pirate writing," Caroline murmured smiling.

"It isn't pirate writing," Nick said. "Look, it says down here, 'See you soon, Uncle Ludovic'. That's not pirate writing."

"The flags probably spell pirate swear words," Caroline said obstinately.

They went outside into a morning so golden that it seemed as if the air around them was stained with the very juice of summer.

The sheep Bunty was kneeling in the middle of a clump of alyssum and virginia stock. She unfolded when she saw the children and bleated in a strange, creaking way.

"She needs oiling, poor old sheep," Nick remarked, scratching the wool between Bunty's neat ears. "Shall we look down on the beach first?"

"It's the only place we know so far," Caroline replied. "We'll start there. Just give him a call first."

"Uncle Ludovic!" Nick called, but his voice sounded too polite and uncertain.

"That's not the way," Caroline said scornfully. She flung her own head back and screamed, "Avast there, Captain. Ahoy! Ahoy!"

But there was no reply. The birds sang on and the sea at the bottom of the track swished and sighed on the sand. Nicholas and Caroline set off down to the beach.

The bay looked different in the morning. The sunshine was all at the other end of the beach, and the sea, curling at the edges to flop onto the sand, was freckled with bright dashes of gold. You could not look at it for long, it was too sharp and sparkling.

"Uncle's boat's still there, anyhow," Nicholas said gladly. He looked up and down the beach for footprints but he could not see any. The stretch of sand was quite clear and smooth as if no one had ever trodden there.

"But the little boat's gone," Caroline replied. "He's gone off to be a pirate in the little boat."

"Wake up, will you!" Nick snapped. "No one could be a pirate in a little boat like that."

"Well, all right then, he's just practising." Caroline refused to give up her idea. "I bet you have to practise being a pirate like you have to practise being a ballet dancer. Ballet dancers have to practise every day or they go all stiff."

"But he said he was trying to give it up," Nicholas said, forced to talk about the pirate story. "He wouldn't go on practising if he was trying to give it up and lead a good life."

Caroline scuffled in the sand. She was wearing clean white socks and brown sandals that filled with sand.

"We'd better go up again," Nick went on. "There's no one here."

But when they turned to go back up the track, dazzled from sun and bright water, Bunty the sheep was waiting at the bottom. She was not looking at Nicholas and Caroline. She was staring past them into the glitter and from behind them came an answering bleat.

"A sea sheep!" Nicholas thought of an animal with the head and front legs of a sheep and the tail of a big fish. But when he turned he saw no sea sheep, only his uncle in little *Sinbad*. His uncle had rowed quietly around the little headland and was making for the beach, he and his boat looking golden in the morning dazzle. Then they came closer and became black and piratical against the brightness of the sea. The children could see the uncle's back and shoulders working easily as he rowed, and a moment after that they heard the gritty sugary sound of a boat nosing up onto a beach. The uncle got out and pulled the boat up higher. Though he had had his back to them he seemed to know they were there.

"Morning!" he said cheerfully. "Sleep well?"

"We thought you were lost," Caroline told him sternly.

"Oh no — impossible. My boats all know the way home. If I happened to go to sleep while at sea little *Sinbad* would always bring me home. Help me pull her up, you crew members. There now! Didn't you get my note?"

"Yes we got it," Nicholas said, "but we couldn't read the flags."

"It said 'Putting out to sea. Back for breakfast'," the uncle explained.

46

"I thought it was pirate swear words," Caroline muttered, rather disappointed at the ordinariness of the message.

"And now to work!" said the Uncle Ludovic. "Up and down the beach collecting wood! We'll light a fire on the beach and cook ourselves some breakfast."

Up and down the beach tumbled Nicholas and Caroline finding wood. Nicholas coming back down the beach found Caroline peering thoughtfully into the little *Sinbad*.

"Look!" She hissed, and Nicholas looking into the back of the boat saw a treasure chest. There was no doubt about it. It was old and battered, but its brass clasps and bands shone splendidly in the sun. It had a big brass lock and its lid fitted on it so tightly, so secretly, that both Nicholas and Caroline knew it must be locked. Nicholas felt shaken. It was impossible to look at a chest like that without believing it was filled with golden coins, rings, jewels and ropes of pearls. He looked around him. The day was certainly very beautiful, but the sand and the sea, the sky and he himself Nicholas, were ordinary after all. Only Uncle Ludovic was strange flickering between being a real uncle and a story-book pirate. Where did the real leave off and the story book begin?

"Come on — don't you want any breakfast!" Uncle Ludovic called, slightly impatiently, like any grown up. He was kneeling over a pile of stones and, as the children came closer, they saw it was a little fireplace. Uncle Ludovic had set a grid over it and from the way the stones and the grid were blackened you could tell he'd cooked out many times before.

Under the grid he had piled crumpled paper, dried grass, dried seaweed like the blackened skeleton of some ancient animal — and some of their sticks.

"Set a match to this," he said.

"Let me! Let me!" Caroline shrieked, but they were both allowed to strike a match and set fire to the paper and dried grass. The flames flared up — almost invisible in the sunlight.

"More sticks," Uncle Ludovic said. "Put a bigger one over the top." Then he did something mysterious. Putting his fingers to his mouth he gave a whistle so shrill that Caroline and Nick breathed in sharply in surprise. The uncle was listening. A moment later a whistle came in reply far away, sweet and clear, like the cry of a witch with the voice of a bird.

The uncle nodded briskly and took off his shirt and blue jeans. He was wearing swimming trunks — red ones — underneath.

"It's in and out of the water all day at this time of year," he said rather shyly.

"Are you going swimming?" Caroline was almost indignant. "Swimming before breakfast?"

"In a way!" Uncle Ludovic replied. "I put a net out very early this morning and now it's time to bring it in. Really I'm going swimming for breakfast. I need another pair of hands however. . . and here they are."

Out of the bush at the other end of the bay came a woman. She was wearing blue swimming togs with a blue-and-white striped towelling jacket. Her hair was in a long fair plait hanging straight down her back. She had very blue eyes and very brown skin

48

and very white teeth. She came towards them with long free strides, a basket in one hand and a blue towel over her shoulder.

"This is Rosie Everest," Uncle Ludovic said. "Her name is really Rosalind, but we call her Rosie. Rosie, this is Nicholas and Caroline."

"Do you live in that red roof up the hill?" Caroline asked. "I mean I know it is really a house but you can only see the roof from here."

"Yes, we're neighbours," Rosie said. She had a wide happy smile, and looked like a person who had lived out in the sun for weeks and weeks.

"We'll just bring the net in," Uncle Ludovic told the children. "Come on Rosie and — you pirates — don't let the fire go out."

"We're not the pirates," said Caroline quickly. "We're the ones helping to reform you of piracy."

"Of course!" Uncle Ludovic replied. "It just slipped my memory for a mere moment."

While Nicholas and Caroline fed the fire Uncle Ludovic and Rosie Everest swam out to the net and began to work it in towards the beach. A long curving line of bobbing corks showed up as the net came inshore. As it came into shallow water Nicholas and Caroline forgot the fire and came running down to the water's edge. They could tell from the splashing that there were fish in the net.

"What's the score?" asked Uncle Ludovic shaking himself like a dog, so that bright beads of water leaped from his hair and beard. "Let's see — six — no, seven flounder, a bottle with no message in it and a rig ——"

"Is that a rig?" asked Nicholas. "It looks like a little shark."

"It is a little shark — but not the man-eating kind," Rosie said.

"They're nice to eat."

"Eat a shark?" Caroline screwed up her nose and shook her head.

"No, you'll like it," Rosie answered smiling. "I'll fillet it and cook it in breadcrumbs. You'll think it's the best fish you've ever had. But this morning we'll have flounder. Throw the two little ones back. The fish that lives to swim away will bigger grow another day."

It was hard to know just what to watch. Uncle Ludovic folding the net up carefully or Rosie preparing the flounders for cooking. In her basket she had knives and forks, a salt shaker, plates with yellow daisies on them, butter, bread and, in a bag of its own, a big black frying-pan. She also had a very sharp knife for scaling and cleaning fish. She was obviously used to managing fish, and within a very short time Nicholas and Caroline were eating fried flounder with a slice of lemon each and the salt shaker between them while two more flounder fried in the pan for Uncle Ludovic and Rosie.

"She's not the cook that I am, though," Uncle Ludovic boasted. "Tomorrow it's her turn to fold the net and my turn to cook."

"It's lovely, though," Nicholas said. "Uncle Ludovic, could I have a try at rowing the boat after breakfast?"

"As soon as you've finished your flounder run up

to the house and put on your swimming togs. Then —
the boat's yours, the sea's yours and the day's yours."

"We live on the beach at this time of year," Rosie
said. "When my daughter Alison's at home we sometimes sleep on the beach on hot nights."

"Where is Alison?" asked Caroline.

"Staying with my sister in the city," Rosie said. "A
holiday is often just a change from what you're used
to and Alison likes to visit a lot of shops for a change.
She's a mermaid for most of the summer."

"I'd like to be a mermaid," said Caroline thoughtfully. "But I can't swim. I keep one foot on the
bottom."

"You'll be a mermaid by the time you leave,"
promised Uncle Ludovic. "Every family with a
pirate in it needs a mermaid too. It balances things
nicely."

And all the time they had breakfast and made each
other promises there was the big sighing breath of the
sea on the sand, with an occasional bleat from Bunty
who did not enjoy fish, but who did not want to be left
out.

6. Hidden Treasure

Over the first two days of the holiday they had spent nearly all their time on the little beach. It had been almost like living on a desert island. Nick was learning to row. Caroline was learning to swim.

"I've got better at swimming," she said. "I used to keep my whole foot on the bottom, but now I only just touch it with my big toe."

"You might as well not touch the bottom at all," Nick replied. "All you need to do is to kick and you will be swimming."

"Well, I just like to know the bottom is still there," Caroline mumbled. "It might suddenly go away." She looked determined. "I'll do it tomorrow. I'll really, truly take my toe off the bottom tomorrow."

"Let's hope you get the chance," Uncle Ludovic

said. "I don't like the look of some of these clouds in the south-west."

"You don't mean it might rain?" asked Nick incredulously.

"It won't rain," Caroline said firmly. "I'm sure of that. No rain." She thought it was always fine at Uncle Ludovic's.

But Uncle Ludovic was right. In the night the wind swung round to the south-west, and when the day came it was grey and angry, biting at anyone who went outside and throwing cold rain at them.

"But what can we do inside?" Caroline cried. "There's nothing to do inside, no toys, no snakes and ladders."

"I know how it is," Uncle Ludovic said very sympathetically. "When I was a pirate wet days were the very devil. We pirates just lay around snarling at each other until the sun came out again. Being a pirate is really a fair-weather occupation."

"Did you ever play snakes and ladders?" Caroline asked.

"Not really — pirates are very superstitious about snakes. And they don't like to play 'Happy Families'. It makes them too sad thinking what they're missing. I suppose you've noticed there's no Mr Patch the Pirate in the 'Happy Families'."

"That's because you can't be happy unless you're good," said Caroline in a very smug voice. And then she sighed. "I'm good," she said mournfully. "But I'm not happy. It isn't fair."

"There's not much justice in this life," Uncle Ludovic said, and found a pack of cards so that they could play "Cheat" and "Snap" and other games. They played for a while and then began to quarrel over who had snapped first. Snap is a good game but it easily leads to hitting.

"Look!" said Uncle Ludovic, hearing the fight and coming out of the kitchen where he had been working quietly. "The rain's eased off. Go and see if there is any mail." Nicholas and Caroline put on windcheaters and went to the letter box, still angry with one another. Bunty the sheep came too, pushing in a wet determined fashion and staring at them with her yellow eyes. She was jealous because they were allowed inside in the wet weather and she was not. There was no mail and on the way back the rain began again. . . not heavy, just cold and unpleasant. At the corner of the house they stopped to listen to the rain water running into the tanks singing a thin echoing song that seemed to have words in it that you could never quite hear.

"It's funny to think of drinking rain," Caroline said thoughtfully.

"Well, rain's just water — we drink it all the time," Nick said sourly, still irritated by the day and the quarrelsome game of "Snap".

"Yes, but this is fresh rain," Caroline replied. "Not old rain that fell down years ago! This rain will be at the top of the tank and we'll drink it first."

"The pipe is at the bottom of the tank, stupid," Nick pointed out. "It'll take us ages to work our way to today's rain — and, anyway," he added doubtfully, "I don't think it works like that. I think it all mixes up in the tank."

55

Caroline held her ear against the tank and laughed. "If you do that," she said, "it sounds like a whole river tumbling into a big lake."

Uncle Ludovic came around the corner of the house, carrying a ladder. He had a sword dangling from his belt and had put on a black leather eye patch, but all he said was, "Get inside or you'll be soaked," just like an ordinary uncle. Nick and Caroline scuttled inside like wet puppies, firmly shutting the door on Bunty who tried to come in too. A moment later Uncle Ludovic came in without the ladder.

"Uncle, you're wearing a sword," Caroline said accusingly. "Are you going back to being a pirate again?"

Uncle Ludovic looked at the sword by his side. "Oh yes, so I am," he said, as if in amazement. "I must have just slipped it on by accident." Then he went back into the kitchen.

"This means more pirate trouble," Caroline muttered to Nick, beginning to look more cheerful. "We'll have to be on the watch."

Even Nick brightened up at the thought of more pirate trouble and watched Uncle Ludovic closely as he went in and out wearing his eye patch and sword, but nothing happened. When you have set your heart on rowing out to the headland, or really swimming for the first time, a day inside is a shock to the system. Nothing else seems as good as what you had planned to do the evening before.

Nicholas tried to read his book, but Caroline, who had nothing to read, was restless and kept annoying

56

him. She lay on her back chanting a list of things in a dull heavy voice: " . . . curtains, picture of a boat, lady with a duck, book case, books, shells, coil of rope, red stone, clock, ship in a bottle, brown armchair. . ."

"What are you on about?" said Nick at last.

"I'm making a list of things in this room," Caroline answered.

"Well, shut up. I'm trying to read."

"That old book! What's happening?"

"They're looking for treasure. They've got a clue — so shut up and let me read," Nick snapped.

Caroline was silent for a moment. "I don't have to," she said at last, in the small careful voice she used for starting an argument.

Just at that lucky moment Uncle Ludovic came into the room.

"Uncle Ludovic — when's lunch?" asked Caroline in a whiney voice.

"Avast there!" Uncle Ludovic grumbled. "That's what I've come to see you about. There's a problem with lunch." Nicholas and Caroline stared at him. "You notice I'm wearing my sword. Well, I must have had an attack of piracy."

"Haven't you cooked lunch?" asked Caroline, staring at him intently.

"Oh yes!" Uncle Ludovic replied. "I cooked it before the piracy attack — but it's gone."

"Gone!" Nick exclaimed. "How can it be gone? Have you eaten it?"

The uncle looked uneasy. "Well, remember I told you — I warned you — that I still had a few pirate habits from time to time? Making people walk the plank! Burying a bit of treasure! All that sort of thing!"

"Have you buried our lunch?" cried Caroline sharply.

"Not to say buried — at least I don't think I've buried it, but I seem to have hidden it."

"Hidden it! Hidden our lunch!" Caroline leaped to her feet. "No lunch?"

"Not unless we can find it," Uncle Ludovic said sadly.

"Why did you do such a thing?" Caroline scolded. "Why didn't you fight against the pirate habit?"

"That's just it. It's a pirate habit," Uncle Ludovic nodded. "Pirates were always hiding treasure and then forgetting where they had buried it. It was really irresponsible behaviour."

"They made maps, though," Nick said slowly with a smile. "Have you made any map?"

Uncle Ludovic looked more cheerful. "That's right, I may have made a map. I'll just have a look round. Would you like to help me?"

"Start in the kitchen," Caroline commanded. "You have spent a lot of time in the kitchen this morning."

There was no sign of a map on the carefully wiped down bench, but on the back of the kitchen door it was easy to see a piece of pad paper with lines written on it in coloured pencil.

"What's that?" asked Caroline, pointing. "It isn't a shopping list is it?"

"Let me see . . ." said Nick. "Chicken in aspic,

59

champagne on ice. . ." It was like a menu for some rich dinner, but then he saw it was a poem.

"Chicken in aspic
Champagne on ice
Cakes full of cherries
All very nice.
Where is it hidden?
Where is it found?
The answer's in pieces
Scattered around.
Find all the pieces
Fit them together
No need to think about
Southerly weather.
A house full of voices
All longing to tell
Where is the lunch
That was hidden so well."

This poem was written in a great number of colours, but underneath it were two lines in blue that said,

"Where is the treasure? The sea nymphs tell.
Hark now I hear them. Ding Dong Bell."

"The bell at the door," cried Nick and Caroline together and nearly trod all over Uncle Ludovic in their rush to get at the ship's bell that hung at his back door.

It was a brass bell, well polished. Nick had never looked at it closely before. Now, as he held it steady, he saw the fine milled edge to its rim, and that someone had engraved two mermaids on it — or were they sea nymphs? Inside the bell, tied to the little chain that held the tongue of the bell, were a piece of paper and a piece of card. As Nick untied them, the tongue of the bell fell against the shining side of the bell and spoke a clear golden word in bell language.

"Let me see! Let me see!" Caroline leaped up and down beside him.

Nick unrolled a piece of paper with another verse on it, and turned the card over. "It's a letter 'H'," he said in a puzzled voice. "Well, let's see what the verse says."

They read it together.

> "The goose girl had a daughter
> And her daughter had a daughter
> And the ladies of this family
> Were really works of art.
>
> And the daughter had a daughter
> And the daughter had a daughter
> And *that* daughter had a daughter
> With a message on her heart."

Nicholas and Caroline stared at each other with frowning faces.

Nick said: "It can't be a real person . . ."

"Rosie's got a daughter," Caroline put in sharply.

"But Rosie's daughter is only about thirteen." Nick shook his head. "And this goose girl must be a great, great, great, great-grandmother. She must be someone really old," (and then he had a thought) ". . . or someone not real at all, because it says the ladies of this family were really works of art. I'm right aren't I, Uncle Ludovic?"

61

"You could be. You could be," said Uncle Ludovic sadly. "My brain's gone numb with hunger and despair."

"You haven't got a picture of a goose girl have you?" Nick asked.

Uncle Ludovic drew himself up tall. "No pirate would stomach a picture of a goose girl in his house," he cried. "We only have pictures of ships and walking the plank."

Caroline suddenly said, "I think I know."

"Know what?" asked Nick.

"I think I know where the goose girl is. I think it's her, though I thought the goose was a duck. It's the lady with the duck in the bookcase."

She dived inside and over to the bookcase, Nick following. At the end of one shelf was a smooth wooden figure painted in bright colours. It was of a woman with a yellow handkerchief over her head and a long red dress with green stripes around the hem. Under one of her painted arms she held a white goose. Nick had never even noticed it before. He picked it up and looked at it. There was a fine crack running right around its waist. Nick shook it gently and it rattled. Caroline's eyes went very wide and excited as Nick carefully twisted the figure in half. The goose girl came into two pieces. It was hollow and inside it was another girl, dressed in the same way, but with a green handkerchief and a yellow dress. And then another one in blue. And another and another and another, each one smaller than the last, and the very last one — a tiny one — had a piece of paper and card tied to it with a rubber band.

62

"Another letter 'H'," Nick said. "We'd better save them."

"It's a short rhyme," Caroline said. And she read,

> "Between the covers a yellow bird
> Sang a song, but wasn't heard."

"Between the covers. . . Uncle Ludovic's bed," shrieked Caroline and raced into his bedroom.

"Hang on! Hang on!" called Nicholas following her.

Uncle Ludovic had a special, very neat way of making beds. Caroline had just pulled the quilt back, but she stopped as Nick bellowed at her. "Think for a moment," he said, "before you wreck Uncle Ludovic's bed. Books have covers too."

"You don't find birds shut in books," Caroline argued.

"You don't find them in beds either," Nick retorted. "But you might find a picture of a bird in a book."

They went back into the living-room.

"There are a lot of books," Caroline said gloomily. "Where shall we start?"

Nick said, "You do the bottom shelf and I'll do the top one and we'll meet in the middle."

There seemed to be no books on birds. Nick noticed that all his uncle's books were on boat building, or the different ways boats had of behaving with different winds and waves. Just the sort of information a pirate might need.

"Any luck?" he asked Caroline, though he knew

she would have shouted out if she had found anything.

"Only books on boats," she replied.

"I'll bet you could actually make a boat, you've got
so many books on boat building," Nick said to his
uncle, as he moved down a shelf.

Caroline moved up one and they met in the
middle.

"No bird books here! All travel books!" sighed
Nick, and leaned back from the shelf frowning.

Directly in front of him was a particularly big
book, dark green with square gold printing on it. You
couldn't miss it — in its gold printing it said, *The
Canary Islands*.

That was it. Just inside the front cover they found
the message and the piece of card with the letter
"H" on it.

> "Shut in the rock for a million years
> I have a message nobody hears
> Won't you please open the red rock door
> And look at the message I have by my claw."

They knew what this was straight away — the
round red stone by the fireplace. Sure enough, when
they looked the rock was really in two pieces. Carefully Nick lifted the top half off. There was the card
with the letter "H" on it. There was the roll of paper
they had come to expect. But there was something
else. Nick stared. Caroline stared. Something
familiar — yet strange.

"What is it? A carving of a crab?" asked Caroline
doubtfully, because how would such a carving get

locked in the rock. "Why is it hidden inside the stone?"

"It's a fossil crab — a million years old," Uncle Ludovic said. "Once he was real, going sideways over and under the stones the way crabs do. Now he's a fossil a million years old."

"A million!" exclaimed Caroline. "A million." She was amazed to think she could look at and touch something as old as that. She smoothed her hand over the rounded dome of the old crab, while Nick picked up the paper to read the rhyme.

"The spider knows
Where the brisk fly goes
And sets his trap with care,
But you can trip
Through the door of the trap
Provided you know it's there."

Nick and Caroline decided that the next clue must be hung in a spider's web somewhere. They looked in the living-room, the kitchen and the bedrooms, but there was no spider's web in sight.

"You're too tidy, Uncle Ludovic," Caroline complained. "A few spiders don't hurt."

"I must have meant something when I wrote that, though," Uncle Ludovic said, "but my memory has faded away — all I can think of is ham sandwiches. Now you think about the bits of card."

Nick set them out on the living-room floor side by side. They were all the same squares of card with the letter "H" on them. They did not mean a thing.

"They're reminding me of something," Caroline

said. "Something we've just seen today without sort of knowing we were looking at it. . . It's something to do with the water tank."

"No, it isn't," Nick exclaimed suddenly. He put the pieces of card one above the other and not side by side.

"It's the ladder," Caroline said. "Uncle Ludovic came round by the water tanks carrying a ladder."

"You use a ladder to go up," Nick reasoned and they both looked at the ceiling. They had already looked there for spider's webs, but this time they saw straight away that there was a trap door in one corner of the ceiling, not easy to see because it was stained the same colour as the ceiling.

"It's a man hole," Nick shouted triumphantly. "Now how did I manage to miss that?"

"You can't trip through the door of the trap without a ladder." Uncle Ludovic got to his feet. "I'd better get it for you. Don't come out — it's raining too hard."

It was raining hard, but Nick and Caroline did not care anymore. Things were too interesting inside for them to bother about the rain. Uncle Ludovic brought the ladder and set it against the wall.

"I hope our lunch is up there," he said anxiously. "I'm really most impressed with the way you've worked it all out — most impressed." He climbed up the ladder as he spoke and pushed the manhole cover away. Then he looked in and gave a cry of joy. "All is well," he cried. "You have a poor uncle's thanks a thousand — no — a million times over."

Caroline was so quick she was several steps up the

ladder before Nick could set foot on it. He had to come after her.

Up under the roof was a little three-cornered room with sloping sides lighted with electric light. It was unlined and you could see the studs of the house like the bones of some large creature holding everything else all together. But it was clean with sea grass matting on the floor. In the middle of the room was a tartan car rug with lunch laid out on it. Ham sand-wiches, biscuits stuck together with icing, hard boiled eggs, lettuce, tomato, cucumber, cheese, a loaf of Rosie's home-made bread and one of Uncle Ludovic's cherry cakes. It was more or less what Uncle Ludovic ate every day, but it was unusual because of being up a ladder in a three-cornered room under the roof and they had had to work to find it. It was a sort of treasure-hunt-attic-picnic lunch.

"It's fun up here," Caroline said, looking around. "What are those books in the corner there?"

"Oh, old books I had as a boy," Uncle Ludovic replied. "Actually, some are older than that. Some of them belonged to your grandfather. And there might even be a few of your father's tucked away."

"Old books of Dad's?" said Nick, wrinkling his forehead.

"Yes, he used to live here with me once upon a time," Uncle Ludovic replied, rather sadly Nick thought, "until he married and got a house of his own."

A lot of thoughts began to chase one another around in Nick's mind while Uncle Ludovic poured out cocoa from a thermos — very welcome for the three-cornered room was not very warm.

There were a lot of things in Uncle Ludovic's house that could be looked at and thought about: the fossil crab that was one whole million years old, the wooden dolls fitting inside one another, so carefully made and beautifully painted, the old books that had belonged to Nick's own father and grandfather. Uncle Ludovic may have been a pirate once but today, turning lunch into a treasure hunt, he was an ordinary uncle trying hard to make things interesting for two children spending a holiday with him. The treasure hunt had been a way of making them notice things for themselves. And yet, with Uncle Ludovic, who could be sure? And why was it so hard to ask? It was easier to ask about one of the other thoughts.

"Uncle Ludovic, why haven't you come to visit us more often?" Nick asked, watching his uncle closely. "I can't remember you coming at all."

"Why haven't we come to visit you till now?" asked Caroline suddenly, begining to think the same thoughts as Nick.

"If our father lived here it's a bit like an ancestral home," Nick went on, thinking of the children in his book. Uncle Ludovic looked up into the studs of the roof. His face seemed to Nick to flicker between real and unreal, between Uncle Ludovic and Pirate Ludovic as it were. Pirate Ludovic won.

"Because of my past wickedness," he answered in a hoarse whisper. "Your mother didn't want you to get mixed up in my villainy until you knew the difference between right and wrong."

"I've known that for ages," said Caroline in a

comfortable voice. "The difference between right and wrong is easy. Right is right and wrong is wrong — that's all there is to it."

"Easier than real and unreal," muttered Nicholas, looking at Uncle Ludovic seriously. "I'm having a lot of trouble telling the difference between what's real and what's a sort of dream."

"I know that too," Caroline shouted, and perhaps she did.

But Uncle Ludovic nodded at Nicholas over the remains of lunch. "So do I!" he said. "So do I!" while the rain poured down on the roof of the ancestral home, rushed along the guttering and fell into the tank, making a tinkling murmuring sound as if the house was having a long wandering conversation with the weather about nothing in particular.

7. The Long White Shed by the Wharf

Though the rain stopped during the night the next day was not very fine. It stayed cool and grey — jersey weather, said Uncle Ludovic, and wore a great brown jersey himself which he told them was knitted out of Bunty's wool. But he had something for them to do, he assured them, something good for a dull day. He put up two trestles and got Nick to help him lift down, from the rafters in his garage, a small canoe.

"It needs a little attention," he said. "It needs to be sanded down and painted for one thing. But it is still water-tight. I've taken good care of it. It used to be your father's when he was small, but he didn't use it for long. He was into a 'P' class and off all over the bay."

"A 'P' class?" asked Caroline. "What's a 'P' class?"

"A little sailing dinghy," Uncle Ludovic answered. "Most kids in New Zealand start off in a 'P' class. I've got ours tucked away in the rafters of the shed. I'll bring it down some other time — when you're a bit more used to water and boats, and you can learn to sail all over the bay too."

"Gosh — that would be great," Nick said.

"The bay?" asked Caroline looking puzzled. She had not really thought of the sea as being shaped into a bay.

"Of course!" said Uncle Ludovic, "Don't you remember seeing it from the top of the hill when we drove over?"

Caroline shook her head. "I don't know," she said. "We got off the bus in a strange place and drove over the hills and came here. We've been here ever since and it doesn't seem like any real place and there doesn't seem to be any proper time — no hours and half-pasts — only day and night. I didn't think we were in a place with any name or shape or south or north or anything."

"It's the holiday feeling," Uncle Ludovic agreed. "Time seems so far off too, when you're just doing what you want when you want to. But this is a real place. There are shops not very far away, and people and money and cars and all the usual things."

"Yes, but where do we get groceries?" Nick said. "Butter and biscuits and things like that! We haven't done any shopping but we get things."

"Pirate magic," said Uncle Ludovic with a grin.

He got sandpaper and wrapped it around blocks of wood. "Rub the canoe down with this," he said. "Rub in the same direction, not all zigzag. Here Caroline, here's one for you. This will probably be your canoe more than anyone else's, so rub hard."

They did work hard too, rubbing steadily, trying not to breathe in the canoe dust that floated into the air. Uncle Ludovic helped and, after a while Rosie came up the path, bringing scones she had made that morning. And she had only been there ten minutes when David Carter, wearing a green jersey and brown corduroy trousers, came down the path from the road.

"I thought I'd come to see how the pirate's reformation was progressing," he said.

"Slowly, slowly I fear," Uncle Ludovic replied with a sigh. "It's uphill work."

"I was hoping some fresh scones might help," Rosie put in.

"A kind thought and worth trying," he replied eagerly.

"Sometimes he seems to be getting a lot better," said Caroline, sticking up for Uncle Ludovic.

Nick watched Rosie and David as they went on discussing his uncle. He thought they might catch his eye and give him a wink but they didn't. They remained serious.

"If you're all going to talk about me as if I wasn't here," remarked Uncle Ludovic grumpily, "I'll go and put the kettle on for tea." He took the teacloth full of warm scones and strode inside, followed by Bunty who meant to stay close to the scones.

"Yesterday he hid our lunch," Caroline said in a gossipy voice. "We had a terrible job finding it, didn't we Nick?"

"Quite fun though," Nick said, standing back from the sandpapering. "We had to follow clues and then climb up a ladder into a sort of attic in the ceiling. But it made us notice a lot of interesting things. He's got a fossil crab that's a million years old. . . " Everyone looked thoughtful.

"A man with a fossil crab can't be entirely bad," David said. "He must have a good side to his nature somewhere. When he pushed me out of the canoe the other day I thought he was a hopeless case, but now I hear about that fossil. . . "

"And look how fond that sheep is of him," said Rosie. "Animals aren't easily fooled you know."

"Bunty would be fooled by anyone giving her scones," Nick said. "She likes scones."

"Here he comes," Nick hissed warningly. "He's made tea for us and buttered the scones." He wanted Uncle Ludovic to get credit for his good deeds.

After tea everyone helped with the sanding of the canoe. Then Rosie and David left and Caroline and Nick helped Uncle Ludovic paint the canoe with special marine paint undercoat.

So the grey day had not been wasted but next morning they woke early with sunshine on the wall filling their room with a mysterious brownish gold light like clear honey. Once again they heard the early morning singing of birds and felt the magical summer holiday feeling that filled them on their first day at Uncle Ludovic's.

Once again they found the house empty and a message in flags and writing from the uncle. They could not read the flags yet, but the writing made itself plain enough.

"If you wake up early and your uncle's gone away
Do not scream the house down. Simply read and play.
Do not ring the hospital. He isn't out of reach.
He'll be coming home again to breakfast on the beach."

"He's a really good poet," Caroline said admiringly. "Let's get dressed and go down to wait for him."

The beach looked quite different from when they had seen it last, for the southerly wind had piled it with sticks and wet mounds of seaweed, and cigarette packets, orange peel and apple cores — rubbish that people had thrown into the sea, perhaps miles away and which the careful water had placed on Uncle Ludovic's strip of sand. There were many seagulls scavenging around the beach — small grey ones with red legs and three huge black backed ones with lemon yellow bills.

"Aren't they tidy?" Nick said. "It looks like a sort of school outing with a lot of boys in absolutely neat school uniform and three teachers in those black gowns professors wear."

"There's been a lot of things washed up," Caroline said. "I expect there's a lot of seagull food been washed up too." She looked around vaguely. "Gosh, a lot of rocks have grown up out of the water," she said.

Nick looked startled for a moment, thinking she might be right. Then he relaxed. "It's the tide," he said. "Don't forget we haven't been down here at this time for two days. The tide must be farther out. It must be almost dead out." The rocks stood strong and dark around the rim of the beach. "You know what?" he went on slowly, "we could walk out to the headland on those rocks."

"Uncle Ludovic said we weren't to," Caroline cried anxiously.

"He said I wasn't to row past the headland," Nicholas corrected her. "But we could walk out there. He didn't say anything about walking over rocks."

"Suppose an octopus comes out of a crack and seizes us," Caroline asked with what seemed to be a real shiver. "I'd hate to die by octopus."

"Look, it's just climbing over rocks like we do at that beach near home," Nick explained patiently, "there won't be any octopuses."

"Octopi," Caroline corrected sternly, "more than one is octopi."

"Yes," Nick answered. "And we'll see Uncle Ludovic if he comes by because we'll have a good view of the whole beach."

There is something magical about rocks and rock pools which are like little complete worlds set in crystal. Once they were started Caroline forgot to worry about any octopus that might be lurking around and enjoyed herself. She wanted to look in every pool and touch every brown anemone to feel them close in their soft ghostly way around her finger. The little stretches of sand between the rocks were like little beaches made in the beginning of the world, new and fresh.

"The rocks are all striped," Caroline said stopping to look.

"That's strata," Nick told her. "That's rock piled up in layers over hundreds and thousands and millions of years."

"We might find a fossil crab a million years old," Caroline cried eagerly.

"We'll look some other time," Nick said, hurrying her on, because suddenly he was filled with excitement at the thought of getting to the end of the headland and seeing what was around the corner, and of seeing the full stretch of the sea. The bay which had been big enough to fill all his thoughts for the last four days suddenly seemed small. He wanted to stand on the headland and look east and south and west, and see nothing but green water.

As they got close to the end of the headland, waves began to break against the rocks, throwing up little showers of spray and foam. Nick was glad he was not in his rowing boat for, though the day was very calm and the waves were not big, they somehow looked powerful and alarming. There were no more little beaches between the rocks, and water appeared lapping impatiently at their feet. They scrambled along, both anxious to reach the headland now.

At last they got there. The sea was as wide and green as Nick had imagined it would be, playful and

threatening all at once, like a lion that might begin by dabbing at a cotton reel you pulled on a string, and just might end by eating you altogether. In front of them there was no land anymore. Nick could not remember ever having seen so much sea. There had always been land on the other side. Caroline must have been thinking the same thing for she said in a small voice, "If we could see far enough would we see Australia?"

Nick was good at seeing maps in his mind. He spent a lot of time at home looking at atlases and encyclopaedias, and liked the sound of the names of far away cities. "I think we're on the wrong side for Australia," he said at last, and began thinking about New Zealand and the great Pacific Ocean.

"But we'd see *some* land," Caroline cried. "We would see some land wouldn't we? It doesn't go on forever like this, does it?" She sounded like someone in a sort of anxious dream.

"We'd see something, stupid," Nick said snappily, because she made him feel uneasy too. "We'd see something because the world is round — probably South America . . . Chile I think." He tried to remember the coast of South America as it was in the big atlas at home. "We'd see Valparaiso and ——" names came into his mind like words of a dimly remembered song "—— and San Ambrosio and — Antofagasta."

Caroline liked the sound of Antofagasta. "Hello, South America," she shouted. "Hello, Antofagasta."

Now that she knew that something was somewhere over the sea she became happy again. Then she turned around. "Oh look! Look at the little bay," she cried.

On the eastern side of the headland lay a tiny bay, just big enough to hold two or three people at low tide. It was perfect with a little curved beach under high rocky banks and small headlands of its own.

"It's mermaid's beach," Caroline declared.

"Mermaids!" exclaimed Nick scornfully, but he scrambled down eagerly after Caroline onto a tiny half moon of sand. There was even a cave into which either he or Caroline could scramble, one at a time. There wasn't room for two. The smell of the sea, the wet rocks and seaweed was enchanting too. Nick began to feel that they might have wandered into some place where time stood still, and that when they returned to real life a thousand years would have gone by. Caroline stood quite still.

"You know what? I'm really happy!" she said solemnly. "Really happy! Usually you don't know you've been happy until afterwards, but I'm happy right now this minute." And she stared at the tiny bay with its rocks and sea and sand as if they were words she was learning by heart.

"Let's see what's on the other side," Nick shouted, and followed by Caroline, he climbed out to see what lay beyond the small bay. Then they got a tremendous surprise.

They were looking into a third bay — much bigger than Uncle Ludovic's, much bigger than the tiny bay behind them. They could see a lot of houses climbing one above the other up the hillside, a shop, a camping ground with caravans and tents in it and a stubby wharf pushing out into the water.

The most noticeable building was a long white shed with a blue roof which ran alongside the wharf and stood out over the sea on piles. Although it was early there were quite a few people on the beach and some even enjoying an early morning swim. On the end of the wharf three men were standing talking, and though it was difficult to tell, for sure, Nick thought that one of them was Uncle Ludovic. He thought he could just make out a beard looking like a doormat.

"How can we get there?" asked Caroline. "There aren't any more rocks for a while."

There was a path with a proper fence that wound round the side of the bay almost to the place where they were standing, but between them and the path was a wall of smooth rock, a little cliff that it would be difficult to cross. Nick looked it up and down. If only they could cross over they would reach the path and be able to hurry around the bay, down the wharf and surprise Uncle Ludovic.

"The cliff flattens out a bit just below the water," he said at last. "There's a sort of ledge. It looks slippery but I think I could get over."

"Well, I can too then," said Caroline. "But you'll have to help me."

"You'd better not try," Nick replied doubtfully. "You can't swim. What if you fell in?"

"You're not to scare me worse," Caroline said in a scolding voice. "I promise I won't get drowned. Just don't leave me behind."

Nick went first. The ledge was fairly easy to walk

along for it was broad and little black mussels clung to it in places so it was not too slippery. The hardest thing was to find places to hang on. Nick, going first, was able to point them out to Caroline. As the water swelled in and out it rose and wet their blue jeans to the knees and they retreated so that their feet were almost out of the water. It gurgled strangely under the rocks, talking in its own language.

As they moved slowly over Nick became more and more nervous — the water was deep. What would he do if Caroline fell in? He couldn't pull her back onto this ledge without falling in himself. In a book he would dive in and rescue her, but would he be able to do this when the rocks were so steep, the bottom so far down and the water wouldn't stand still?

But Caroline did not fall and they reached the path in safety. They ran quickly onto the beach and towards the wharf and the big white shed. The three men were coming down the wharf as the children came up it, and Nick could see that for once they had really surprised their uncle. He looked very worried as well as surprised and came towards them quickly.

"Are you okay?" he asked. "Is everything all right?"

"It's fine," Nick replied. "Nothing's wrong! The tide was so low that we were able to walk round."

"It must have been a bit risky out at the head-land," Uncle Ludovic remarked, looking rather sternly at Nick. "You know Caroline can't swim."

"Not being able to swim made me very careful," Caroline said.

"I don't know," said Uncle Ludovic. "How do

fathers get on? I don't want to be cross, but I think I ought to be."

Nick, looking up over Uncle Ludovic's square shoulder, blinked and looked again. There, on the white shed, he saw his own surname — BATTLE painted in very heavy black letters. He could scarcely believe it until he read the two smaller words, one above it and one below: "Ludovic BATTLE, boat-builder."

"Uncle Ludovic," he cried, "you're a boatbuilder." He remembered the rows of boat-building books in the shelves at home. "You're a boatbuilder all the time."

"Some of the time!" said Uncle Ludovic looking less stern. "I'm on holiday at present like you."

"A boatbuilder," cried Caroline indignantly. "What about being a pirate?"

"Well, it's quite possible to be both at once," Uncle Ludovic replied. "Besides, if I want to give up piracy it's very handy to have an honest trade to step into, isn't it? I want to use my talents for the good of the world."

"I didn't know you'd got as far as this," Caroline said. "Are these other men boatbuilders too — or are they pirates?"

"One of them works with me," Uncle Ludovic replied. "That's Murray Morgan here. And the other man, the one with the sandy hair and freckles, is the man we're building a boat for. His name's Jeff — Jeff Morpeth — and he's a big man in this town because he runs the shop — in between sleeping and swimming."

"Go on! Don't you believe him," said Jeff Morpeth. "I'm working flat out this time of year."

"I'll bet you are if you sell ice cream," Caroline replied seriously. "Do shopkeepers eat a lot of their own ice cream?"

"I do take a bit from time to time," Jeff Morpeth said. "I'll send a block home with your uncle tomorrow morning if I remember. There's no doubt it's good ice cream weather."

"Can we see inside the shed?" Nick asked his uncle. For once he was not interested in ice cream.

"Tomorrow morning would be better. I'll wake you up and you can come with me. I just take a quick trip over to check up on things and then, at present, the rest of the day's my own. But we won't have time to have a good look now. Rosie will be expecting us for breakfast at any moment. Little *Sinbad* is drawn up on the end of the wharf so come on. We'll row back."

The first thing Nick and Caroline saw when they climbed into little *Sinbad* was the treasure chest they had seen on their first morning.

"Go on — ask him," Caroline signalled,

"Not our business," Nick signalled back.

"I will then!" said Caroline's funny fair eyebrows, and she asked, "Uncle Ludovic — what's in that box? Is it treasure?"

Deep in his beard Uncle Ludovic's smile shone secretly. "Treasure of a sort," was all he said. "You can open it when we get home."

The water talked along the sides of the boat as they went along. Then after a while the swell began to move under them.

"What if it was rough?" Nick asked. "Wouldn't you be able to go to work?"

"I'd drive over of course. It's quicker to drive anyway. But I like rowing and I like the look of the water on a calm day, so I go the slow way."

"It's the first time we've seen your bay from out here," Caroline remarked, "looking in at the beach and not out from it. It's nice." The water was like green glass. The hills, the little jetty, the rocks — all had reflections slightly misty around the edges.

"Is it really your bay?" Caroline asked.

"No one can own a bay in this country," Uncle Ludovic replied, "but it seems like mine. I was the first person to live here you know. Now Rosie's got a house too, of course, and there are two other weekend places at the other end of the beach — see, over there. There's a track down from the road, but not many people come down it. Most people head for the big bay — there's a shop you see, with ice creams and hot water for babies' bottles. And there's more shade. We don't get too many visitors yet."

"Are you glad?" asked Caroline.

"I don't mind company, but ——" Uncle Ludovic paused, and laughed a little. "Yes, I am glad. We pirates come to appreciate a bit of stillness as we get older."

Nick said nothing. He watched green glass water curling out in wide ripples that were spreading out behind them. Suddenly the world had opened out for them — Uncle Ludovic's bay wasn't the only bay any more. It had a place. It belonged in a real world, and so did Uncle Ludovic. He was a boatbuilder. Still,

Nick thought, even if Uncle Ludovic wasn't a pirate and perhaps never had been, he was a very unusual person. You never knew what he would do next, but you knew it would be fun. There ought to be a name for someone as special as he was — not pirate, because he wasn't wicked, but some word rather like it.

When they landed on the beach Caroline called out, "The treasure chest, Uncle! Don't forget the treasure chest!"

So Uncle Ludovic had to open its brass catches and tilt back its rounded heavy lid. Nick and Caroline almost banged heads as they bent over it, peering in.

It was full of tools, a hammer, a 'T' square with a little spirit level set in the handle, screwdrivers, chisels, different sizes of spanner. But on the very top were two pounds of sausages and a pound of butter.

"No fish today," Uncle Ludovic said. "I didn't set a net. Besides we pirates get very sick of fish you know and dearly love the occasional sausage. Many a pirate I've known would swap a bag of rubies for a single fried sausage."

"Gosh I wouldn't," Caroline said.

"In some parts of the world, sausage sellers are richer than pirates," Uncle Ludovic said with a sigh. "Now how about some firewood, and I'll whistle to let Rosie know we've arrived safely."

8. Parties

The next two days were so calm and fair that Uncle Ludovic took the children out each day in the big *Sinbad*, and they sailed down the coast visiting other bays and inlets and coming home in the long light evenings. They anchored in quiet spots and the children fished while Uncle Ludovic cooked sausages on the little stove in big *Sinbad*'s cabin. The cabin was very small but interesting with a folding table as well as the stove, and seats with cupboards under them where Uncle Ludovic kept tea, tinned milk, biscuits and several cans of soup. Around the wall were Uncle Ludovic's certificates, entitling him to navigate coastal shipping or even a tug if the need should arise.

"I don't need certificates to sail big *Sinbad*," Uncle

Ludovic explained. "Big *Sinbad* is just a pleasure craft, but I like to keep them — one never knows just what is going to come up someday."

So Uncle Ludovic's world began to open up around them. Pirate questions were put aside for a while. There was so much else to think about, even Caroline was willing to forget pirate things for a day or two. As for Nick, he found himself wondering more and more why this useful uncle had been hidden away for so long. Why hadn't he visited them more often? Why hadn't they visited him? "Wickedness," his uncle had said, but that was only his pirate answer.

The canoe was painted and left on its trestles to dry. Caroline learned to swim a few strokes, taking her toe off the bottom at last. Loving postcards arrived from Australia. Nothing stood still. Time came back into their lives and days started to be counted once more. Eight days — just over a week — they had been with Uncle Ludovic, and their parents would be home in eight days more.

"We're just halfway," Caroline remarked mournfully. "It's Monday today and they're coming back next Monday. It doesn't seem long."

"We can do a lot of things in eight days," Nick pointed out.

"We'll have to work terribly hard to reform Uncle Ludovic of piracy in eight days," Caroline went on. "I don't think we're getting on quickly enough. Rosie's having people round tomorrow, mind you. That might help."

Nick, who had been thinking of launching the

canoe was irritated. "It's just a game all that pirate business," he snapped. "It's just a game they're playing."

Caroline stared at him gravely. "Well, even if it is a game," she said, "it's a game they're playing with us and not against us. Being a game isn't important. Even in *games* you try to win, and I want to win this one. What about that book of yours? Has it got any useful ideas we could copy?"

"I finished it," Nick said, not liking to be reminded that he had felt so strange about the book a few days before. "It isn't anything to do with what's going on here — not really."

"Well, I'm going to read it," said Caroline. "Even if I can only read bits of it I might find some clue about what to do next."

It was true that on the following day, a Tuesday, Rosie was giving a lunch party in the red roofed house across the bay. Of course Uncle Ludovic, Nicholas and Caroline were invited, but none of them was prepared for any sort of unexpectedness beforehand. They had breakfast inside and not on the beach because Rosie was tidying the house for visitors and besides it gave them a chance to taste porridge again. While Uncle Ludovic and the children were eating it sprinkled with brown sugar and thinking it tasted quite different after a week without it, the door burst open and Rosie herself came in. She had a sheet over one arm and two pairs of scissors in her hand. "Ludovic Battle!" she cried. "Your time has come."

Uncle Ludovic looked at her in great apprehension. "Just what do you have in mind?" he asked, putting his coffee cup down carefully.

"If you really want to give up your piratical ways and reform," Rosie declared, "you'll have to begin by trimming your beard."

"No, no!" cried Uncle Ludovic leaping to his feet, but Caroline grabbed his arm.

"It's true, Uncle," she declared. "I didn't think of that. Get your beard off at once."

"Not all of it," added Rosie reassuringly. "Just a bit of it, to shorten it, give it some shape. It looks as if you'd glued a possum skin to your face at present."

"It really does," said Caroline with a giggle. "Get it made all neat and tidy, Uncle, then you'll feel much less like a pirate. All your pirate thoughts might be coming from your beard."

"I'll lose my strength if you cut my beard," Uncle Ludovic declared. "I'll go all weak."

"No you won't, I promise," Rosie said. "Just think — if you want to get into good society your whiskers must look respectable. Don't be afraid. It doesn't hurt a bit."

"Afraid?" cried Uncle Ludovic.

"It will be just like Bunty getting shorn," Rosie said. "Bunty didn't make such a fuss."

"I like your whiskers, Uncle Ludovic," said Nick. Then a thought came to him. "People say that if whiskers are cut they grow again, but a lot thicker."

"Do they? Do they say that?" asked Uncle Ludovic eagerly. "Well, in that case, I'll let you trim me a bit, but nothing serious mind you."

"No, and don't forget, Ludovic, my mother will be

there and she disapproves of beards at the best of times," Rosie said.

So Uncle Ludovic had to sit in a chair while Caroline tucked the sheet around his neck. Then he had to tilt his head back while Rosie began to trim his beard. She snipped and snapped around him and big pieces of beard began to fall to the ground.

"Get his hair brush and comb," Rosie commanded Caroline, who ran off to Uncle Ludovic's bedroom to get these necessary things. "I'll trim his hair too, while I've got him at my mercy."

Uncle Ludovic groaned a bit.

"Don't worry Uncle," Caroline patted his shoulder. "You'll suddenly go all handsome. It's worth the trouble."

When Rosie was finished and Uncle was clipped, brushed and combed and his sheet was whisked away, he certainly looked a changed man. He still looked unusual, but unusual in a tidy way.

"I feel light-headed," he said, picking up the shiny teapot and looking at his reflection in it. "Ugh! is that me?"

"You can't tell by looking at yourself in a teapot," Caroline cried scornfully. "Your nose goes all big, and your eyes go all slitty and your forehead sort of disappears. You don't really look like that Uncle Ludovic."

"I'm glad," said Uncle Ludovic simply. "It would be a heavy price to pay for social success."

Rosie said goodbye. "See you at 12.30. Don't forget."

"Your invitation is engraved on my heart," said

Uncle Ludovic politely. "In the meantime may we go about our simple maritime duties?"

"Yes, you may — but don't turn up with bare feet. Caroline, I'm relying on you to see that he looks suitable."

The three of them went down to the beach followed by Bunty. Caroline lay on the beach reading Nick's book while Uncle Ludovic and Nick went around the bay, swimming and rowing little *Sinbad*, turn and turn about.

They went home again in plenty of time to dress for Rosie's party.

Mrs Battle, the mother of Nick and Caroline, had packed best clothes for each of them, being the sort of person who cannot imagine a holiday without a lot of dressing up. So Caroline wore her long blue gingham dress with the pin tucks and the daisy braid, and Nicholas wore his bottle green shirt, long fawn trousers, dark brown shoes and belt. They both admired themselves very much indeed after eight days of wearing beach clothes often damp and sandy around the edges, and they both enjoyed getting dressed up with a party ahead of them. But they admired Uncle Ludovic even more when he appeared wearing his coffee coloured corduroy trousers, and a very elegant brown suede jacket that exactly matched his brown suede shoes. His hair was brushed, his beard was combed and he suddenly looked rather like his brother Andy Battle, father of Nick and Caroline, only shorter and older.

"Gosh! I'd never have known you," Nick cried.

"Respectability often seems to mean dressing

92

warmly," was all Uncle Ludovic said, pulling a face. "Do you think I'll do Rosie credit?"

"She'll be really pleased," Caroline said earnestly.

Rosie's house had a long verandah facing the sunny northwest, and when they arrived several people were sitting there already, drinking and talking. At the sight of them Bunty stopped and bleated stamping her feet. Uncle Ludovic and the children had to push past her onto the lawn Rosie had cut only the day before. Bunty watched jealously from the shade of a native fuchsia.

Rosie came to meet them looking very elegant and gracious. She was wearing a long navy and white cotton dress, crisp and summery in the lunch-time sun. Her fair hair, which she usually wore in a plait, was shining as if it had been brushed a hundred times and was pinned up in a golden twist on the back of her head so that, suddenly, she looked very tall and beautiful and even Caroline began to look shy. However, when she smiled, it was still the same old Rosie looking amused at all the glory of best clothes and brushed hair her party was bringing out into the open.

"Would you like a drink?" she asked in a proper way and brought the children long glasses full of orange juice and lemonade with iceblocks and borage flowers floating on the top. It was the prettiest drink Nick and Caroline had ever had, pretty to look at with the blue borage, pretty to listen to, with tinkling ice and the tiny prickling fizz of lemonade. Uncle Ludovic had whisky, though Caroline nudged him disapprovingly and said that he shouldn't drink strong drink in case his pirate ways came to the fore again.

Rosie's party was really a grown-up party, though there were two babies (one very young asleep in a carry cot in the bedroom) and a boy a little older than Nick. His name was Oswald Sherman but everyone called him Occie.

David Carter was there, wearing his proper minister's clothes but he could not stay long. Murray Morgan the man who helped Uncle Ludovic with boatbuilding was there and so was Jeff Morpeth the shop man from the bar around the headland. He had meanly left a cousin of his to look after the shop in case anyone wanted petrol or ice-creams. There was the man who drove the Rural Delivery van bringing letters and bread to people's places every morning, and a cheerful woman who turned out to be a nurse. It seemed as if everyone in the two bays, Uncle Ludovic's bay and the bay next door, was having a pleasant time on Rosie's summer lawn. Everyone knew everyone else and there was none of that awkward time of quiet, stiff talk that you sometimes get at parties where people have to get to know each other.

Rosie's mother, Mrs Russell, who had come over from town and did not seem to know many of the local personalities sat on a chair on the verandah. She did not go out to talk to other people. They had to come up and talk to her. Caroline heard her say to Rosie, "Everyone seems to be enjoying themselves I must say, though it seems very strange to me, dear, to see you here like this, when I think of some of the wonderful opportunities you had in the old . . ."

"Oh, for goodness sake, mother!" Rosie exclaimed, "Don't you see I love it here — I'm happy."

"You certainly look very well, dear — very *brown*," said Mrs Russell rather sourly, and she sighed like someone who is putting up with a good deal.

And Nick, who was with Uncle Ludovic when he stopped to talk to Mrs Russell, could see quite clearly that Mrs Russell did not like Uncle Ludovic even though his beard was clipped. Nick could tell by her careful, polite way of speaking, and by her smile which curled the corners of her mouth but did not touch the rest of her face. However, when she smiled at Caroline her eyes grew warm and crinkled up at the corners, so you could see Mrs Russell could smile when she wanted to.

The mysteriousness of grown-up life and the feeling of a lot of things going on over his head made Nick rather tired of the party, and he was glad to go off with Occie Sherman, down to the beach to show off the two *Sinbads*. Caroline stayed, she said, to watch Uncle Ludovic in case of pirate behaviour. Really she was enjoying the party and the magical feel of a long dress swishing around her heels after so many days of shorts and blue jeans.

When Nick and Occie Sherman came up from the beach Mrs Russell had gone and other people were going home too. Rosie's party was over, thought Nick. But he was wrong. After Rosie had shouted and waved goodbye to the Shermans (and he had shouted and waved too), the sound of music began to nibble at the edge of his hearing, real music, not the practised tinned sort you get from the radio. He followed it to the kitchen where he found the party had started again, still the same party, but smaller and closer and easier than before.

Murray Morgan and Jeff Morpeth sat on the kitchen table with their feet on kitchen chairs. Uncle Ludovic leaned against the refrigerator and Jenny Morpeth, Jeff's pretty wife, sat on a stool playing the guitar and singing in a voice as dark as the bush in the hills. Perched on a clear edge of the kitchen bench, swinging her heels, was Caroline, while the Morpeth baby staggered around on its fat legs sitting down plump on its napkin, every now and then. When Jenny Morpeth played a tune that everyone knew, everyone sang.

"Hello, Nick," Uncle Ludovic called across the kitchen. "Come to join the dishwashing and clean-up squad?"

"If we help with the dishes we're allowed to eat what's left over," Caroline told him. "It's a pirate rule for dishwashing parties."

It was strange that washing the dishes should turn out to be part of the party — and the best part too. Rosie came in with a pile of tea towels and a big striped butcher's apron which she made Uncle Ludovic wear.

"It really suits you," Murray Morgan said. "You ought to wear one all the time."

Caroline watched Uncle Ludovic closely, frowning to herself. Then she pulled at Nick's sleeve. "I finished that book of yours this morning," she hissed. "You didn't tell me it finishes with the smuggler uncle marrying the squire's daughter."

"Oh well, that was just the usual happy end," Nick said — the book seemed far away — not very important — as if it was a book someone else had read last year. "I'm going sailing with Occie Sherman tomorrow," he boasted. "Occie's got a 'P' class sailing dinghy."

"But you said nothing happened," Caroline hissed again.

"Well, nothing did happen did it?" Nick replied scornfully. "Nothing to do with us."

"Yes it did! The uncle got married and gave up smuggling," Caroline whispered.

"Occie's got a spare life jacket. I think Uncle Ludovic will let me go." Nick did not have space in his mind for the book any more. His thoughts were already filled with boats and the sea.

For some reason the food that was left over had started to taste more delicious than it had, properly served, during the day. Perhaps the music and the singing made a difference or the easy feeling of the house settling back on itself now the party was over.

"This is the sort of party pirates have," Caroline announced dreamily eating with her fingers.

"And it's really time I got you home and tucked you into bed," Uncle Ludovic replied, "because it's starting to get dark, and by the time you're washed and brushed and polished and all that the stars will be out."

Rosie came across to the lawn with them to the begining of the track between the two houses. She smiled and yawned and smiled again, gave them a hug each and started to go back towards the house.

Suddenly Caroline ran back after her, putting up her arms as if she wanted another hug. But when Rosie bent down to her Caroline began whispering in her ear.

"What was that?" Uncle Ludovic and Nick heard Rosie ask, sounding amused and surprised. Caroline whispered again — hissing in a serious, anxious way. Then Rosie straightened up and laughed.

"I quite agree with you," she said. "It might be the saving of him. I'll think about it and let you know." And then she waved and smiled again and went back across the lawn to her open door while Uncle Ludovic led the children home. Bunty met them bleating and stamping her feet, butting reproachfully because they had left her alone all afternoon, but there was not time to play with Bunty. They were taken in, showered, pyjamad, hair brushed, teeth brushed, and tucked into bed where they were pleased to be, because they were both very tired and bed was kind to their tiredness.

The phone rang. Was it late or early? Nick woke anxious in case it should be some message from his faraway parents. The bedroom door was not quite shut and Nick heard Uncle Ludovic's voice clearly as he answered the phone.

"Yes?" he said cautiously. Then his voice sounded amused as he said, "For goodness sake!" He listened for a minute and when he spoke again his voice had changed again. He sounded excited and anxious. "Look I'll come over." Then he said, "Next *week*! Are you sure?" Then he listened for quite a long time. "All right," he said at last, "that's best. We'll talk about it tomorrow early. And listen — sweet dreams."

Nick heard the click of the phone as it was put down. Then silence. "Is everything all right?" he called, still thinking of his parents in Australia. Uncle Ludovic bounced into the little room. He looked distracted and hugged Nick with the sort of big bear hugs that Nick's father used to give him. He looked as if he had been given an amazing present that might break to pieces if he did the wrong thing.

"Everything is fine," he said. "Sleep well." Then he bounced out again. Even after the light was out and the door closed Nick could hear him singing softly to himself and walking around the room next door like a lion in a cage of dreams.

9. All Questions Answered But One

The moment Nick opened his eyes in the morning he knew that something in the house had changed. He had a feeling that things would not be as they had been though he didn't know why. Everything *seemed* the same as usual and somewhere in the next bay Occie Sherman was waiting with a spare life jacket. Nick got up and had a rather hurried breakfast before he set out with Uncle Ludovic in little *Sinbad,* while Caroline went over the bush path to Rosie's place.

It was a good morning, sailing with Occie, though Nick felt more like an explorer on the moon when he put on the spare life jacket. It was rather too large for him and was one of the puffy sort making it awkward to move quickly until you were used to it. Nevertheless Nick was glad of it when a sudden gust of wind caught the sail and the little yacht keeled over. It was easy to get it righted again and, later in the morning, Occie turned it over twice on purpose so that Nick could try righting the boat himself and climbing back into it.

"You're not a sailor until you've canned out about a thousand times," Occie shouted, water pouring down his face from his wet hair. "Lucky we don't go rusty!"

But at last the sailing was over. Occie and his father drove Nick home and put him off at Uncle Ludovic's letter box.

Everyone was out. The house was very quiet. Nick went on down to the beach expecting to find Uncle Ludovic and Caroline there, but the little beach was quite empty except for seagulls.

He walked back to the house as Uncle Ludovic came down the path from the garage. He soon realized it was Uncle Ludovic who made things feel different. He talked and behaved like a stranger copying the Uncle Ludovic of yesterday — almost the same but not quite. Nick could tell he was really thinking hard about something else. And when Caroline came home from Rosie's, she had a secret.

Caroline really enjoyed secrets. She did not tell them, but she looked all puffed up and pleased with them, holding her lips tightly together in case the secret slid out by accident, and thinking carefully about her words. She had a way of looking at Nick that reminded him all the time that she knew something that he didn't. It was very irritating. Straight after lunch she set off back to Rosie's again, wearing her pink linen dress and socks and shoes as if she was going out. Nick began to feel rather grumpy. Later he went out and worked on the canoe with Uncle Ludovic who said it needed yet another coat of paint before it was ready for launching. But for the first time since he came to visit Uncle Ludovic Nick felt bored and uneasy. Something more important than canoes was going on and he was not part of it.

They had been stirring and scraping for about half an hour when the phone rang. Nick, who was inside collecting an old knife from the kitchen drawer, answered it. It was a cable from Australia, but it was for Uncle Ludovic not him. He had to call his uncle and wait to see if there was any message.

It was not bad news: Uncle Ludovic laughed and looked pleased. He saw Nick staring at him.

"That was from your father," he said. "They'll be home on Monday."

"We already knew that," Nick replied in a grumbling voice, beginning to stir a pot of white paint that needed to be thoroughly mixed.

"They were just making sure," Uncle Ludovic said in an absent-minded way.

Nick stood up letting his stick droop and weep tears of white paint onto the green grass.

"What's going on?" he cried. "Things are getting all different. Everything has changed since yesterday. Caroline knows about it and I don't. It's not fair."

Uncle Ludovic seemed startled and looked at Nick as if he was really seeing him for the first time that day.

"Gosh, I'm sorry," he said. "The fact is it's a very

upside down day for me too. And that's why I'm not thinking very clearly about being a good uncle today. But there's no secret. Not really. You see for a long time now I've wanted to get married to Rosie Everest, but she hasn't been sure she wanted to marry me. But last night after the pirate supper, she rang up and said she thought it was a good idea and how about a wedding a week from yesterday — next Tuesday."

"Next Tuesday!" cried Nick.

"Yes — it takes a lot to surprise me, Nick, but Rosie has filled me with astonishment, and that's why I am so vague today. I've had a frantic morning. The first thing was to send a cable to your parents in Sydney, to make sure they would get here. Then I rang up David to see if he would have time to marry us on Tuesday — it's very useful having a minister for a friend, but David has a big parish and leads a busy life. Fortunately he can fit us in on Tuesday so we'll make it a morning wedding with lunch for our guests."

"Almost like yesterday," said Nick in a pleased voice.

"Well — almost!" Uncle Ludovic nodded. "So that was decided. And then, while you were sailing around with Occie I had to drive over to town and get the application to marry from the Justice department. Rosie and I signed it and she's taking it back this afternoon because it has to be lodged there for three full days before the wedding. So you see I've had a morning full of distractions."

"It's a bit of a rush isn't it?" asked Nick. "People

104

usually take longer over weddings."

"Well, I don't like to argue," Uncle Ludovic said, "in case Rosie changes her mind. I've had a dreadful job getting her to agree as it is. And then we have to have you and Caroline as guests. It seems Caroline thinks the whole thing is her idea. Apparently last night, just as the pirates were leaving, Caroline whispered to Rosie that someone ought to marry me to save me from more piracy. She thought I might be redeemed by the love of a good woman."

"Oh," Nick cried in a disgusted voice. "It's that book — a book I brought with me about two children staying with a smuggler uncle. Some things in the story seemed like some things that were happening to us, only you were a pirate uncle, not a smuggler, you see. I suppose, when the uncle got married in the end of the book, Caroline thought it would match nicely if you got married too. She was worried you wouldn't be cured of piracy before we left and she hates leaving things not finished."

"Well she's certainly hit on a good way of making sure I behave from now on," Uncle Ludovic replied. "She's very thorough, isn't she?"

Nick began stirring the paint again. "Rosie wouldn't marry you just because of what Caroline said," he remarked thoughtfully. "She must have made up her mind before that."

"Goodness, I hope so," Uncle Ludovic answered cheerfully. "But the thing is Rosie was married before, you know, and things went wrong for her as they sometimes do. It's made her think very carefully about getting married again. That's all."

"What sort of things went wrong?" asked Nick, delighted at getting the answers to some questions he had not even got round to asking yet.

"It's hard to say really," Uncle Ludovic said. "Her husband was very successful and made a lot of money. You'd think that would be good, wouldn't you? But it changed their lives a lot, and Rosie didn't enjoy a lot of travelling and entertaining. She likes picnics and fishing and sailing. There wasn't time for any of the things that she enjoyed when her husband became so busy and successful. They argued a lot and made each other unhappy. At last Rosie and Alison came back to live here, and Rosie's husband went up to Auckland. But that was a long time ago."

"She won't quarrel with you, I'm sure," Nick said confidently.

"She'd better not!" declared Uncle Ludovic sternly. "That would be disastrous. We can't afford to be distracted by arguments when we're planning a sailing career together. I've wanted a crew for my keeler for a long time and Rosie's a very good sailor."

"She might want to be Captain," Nick said.

"Do you think so?" Uncle Ludovic shook his head. "I'm better in a keeler than she is, though I think she'd beat me hands down in a Moth these days. However if she wants to be skipper sometimes she can be and I can't say fairer than that."

Nick laughed and began wiping his paintbrush on a turpentiney rag. His mind was whirling with new things to· think about and one particular thought bobbed like a cork to the surface of his thoughts. "Will Mrs Russell be pleased?" he asked and Uncle

Ludovic looked grave.

"No," he admitted. "She rather liked Rosie's first husband and I'm a very different sort of person. And not only that, Mrs Russell really liked the travelling and the parties and the hair sets and all the things that Rosie got tired of doing. She can't understand why Rosie didn't enjoy them too. Members of the same family are sometimes a great puzzle to one another."

"Sometimes you're a puzzle to me," Nick said boldly. "There are a lot of things I don't understand."

"Like what for instance?" asked Uncle Ludovic cautiously.

"Well, like, have you quarrelled with my mother or father?" Nick asked. He felt he could ask Uncle Ludovic anything in this co-operative mood.

"They wouldn't send you on holiday with someone they've quarrelled with," Uncle Ludovic replied cunningly.

"Yes, but why haven't you ever been to visit us — since we were babies anyway?" Nick cried. "And why haven't we been to visit you?"

"Well, I've been at sea a bit —" Uncle Ludovic replied, "— on the South-East Asia run — and then I did a few months on the Cook Strait Ferry." He paused and Nick looked at him hard. "All the same," said Uncle Ludovic, "I know what you mean, and I'm shy of answering because you make me think of a time when I behaved rather like Mrs Russell."

"You did?" Nick stared at him doubtfully.

"It was like this . . ." Uncle Ludovic began. "I'm

a lot older than your father — ten years in fact. Our mother died when your father was very small and I used to look after him when I came home from school. He was my afternoon job. And I looked after him altogether when our father died. I was twenty then and at sea on a cargo boat. I flew home I remember. We sold the town house and came here to live. This place had been our weekend holiday house, but Andy and I lived here for years." Uncle Ludovic sighed and smiled. "We got on well. I was really happy a lot of the time. . . and gosh, the things I learned to do. I learned to cook and I worked with the man who ran the boatbuilding business — the same shed I've got now. I did a lot of sailing and I learned to knit. . ."

"Knit!" exclaimed Nick blinking.

"Yes. I got second prize at the local show for a green jersey I knitted for Andy — a dark green jersey in fisherman cable. I got good at knitting. Andy, your father, was a very easy-going boy. He always did what I told him. Perhaps that was the trouble."

"What was the trouble?" asked Nick.

"I turned into a sort of Mrs Russell with a beard," Uncle Ludovic sighed. "I thought that what was best for me was best for Andy. I thought I knew just what was best for him. I wanted him to go into the boat-building business with me."

"Dad a boatbuilder!" cried Nick. He could not imagine it.

"There you are. I couldn't believe he might prefer cars and the city and to run a business of his own," Uncle Ludovic mumbled. He took the paintbrush from Nick's hand, and gently straightened its bristles. A narrow trim ran around the top edge of the canoe. Uncle Ludovic began to paint very delicately. After a moment he went on, "Of course there wasn't any real argument until after your father got engaged and then married. Your mother had some pretty strong ideas of her own and, believe me, Nick, they didn't include the bay, or boatbuilding or me." Uncle Ludovic laughed. "Well, we didn't actually quarrel but we must have come close to it a dozen times. And at last I saw your poor father was caught between two people both telling him what he ought to do, and I decided I wouldn't visit quite so often." Uncle Ludovic was silent. Nick nudged him to go on. Uncle Ludovic picked up a scrap of painting rag and wiped a little smear away from the blue part of the canoe.

"Never joggle a painting man," he said reprovingly. "And then I went back to sea and got my second mate's ticket. I used to stay here when I came home and I kept in touch — kept my hand in at boatbuilding too, so that when the boatbuilder retired I left the sea and took the business over. And that's the story of my life and how I turned from an interfering Mrs Russell into the lovely pirate I am today."

Nick knelt beside the canoe, nodding slowly. He found he could imagine his mother being suspicious of Uncle Ludovic and his father trying to please both of them. He felt alive with new thoughts and understandings as the pieces fitted together in his mind. Almost all his questions were answered. There was only one left.

"I don't suppose we'll be seeing much of Caroline from now on," Uncle Ludovic went on. "Rosie says she wants two bridemaids — her daughter Alison for one and Caroline for the other — and she's taken Caroline to town with her to collect Alison and to buy some dress material."

"Caroline will like being a bridesmaid," Nick said thoughtfully.

"Well, that gave me an idea," Uncle Ludovic said. "I've asked your father to be my best man, but if Rosie has two bridemaids why shouldn't I have two best men, and why shouldn't you be one? You can look after the ring and hand it to me when I need it. Your father will sign as a witness to our marriage. I think that's all there is to do."

"Gosh, I'd like that," Nick said gruffly. "Would I have to dress up though?"

"It's not that sort of wedding really," Uncle Ludovic said. "Just what you wore yesterday will be fine. And Nick — don't tell Caroline that you're going to be one of my best men — then you can have a secret too."

Nick grinned. After a minute he said,"It's been a very good time for answering questions this afternoon. All my questions are answered — all except one."

"Nick you chill my blood," Uncle Ludovic declared. "What with Caroline bossing me and you asking difficult questions I'm going to be a broken man by Tuesday next. You and your father will have to carry me to the altar on a stretcher. What's your last question?"

"Will you tell me truly and no tricking?" Nick asked.

"No tricking!" Uncle Ludovic agreed.

Nick took a deep breath. "Uncle, in all your travelling, were you ever really a . . . were you ever really truly a . . . ?" Suddenly Nick stopped.

"Yes?" said Uncle Ludovic, looking at him, waiting, half smiling.

"Nothing!" Nick said at last. "I've decided not to ask."

"Quite right," Uncle Ludovic remarked approvingly. "There should always be some unanswered questions. Life would be dull if it was all answers."

Nick still frowned surprised to find that he did not want to know whether or not Uncle Ludovic had ever, just possibly, really been a pirate.

"Life might get dull for you," he said, "giving up travelling and getting married."

"Nick!" cried Uncle Ludovic solemnly. "Getting married for the first time when you're over forty is the most dangerous adventure you can imagine. And don't forget I've still got to make Mrs Russell like me. I've got plenty of adventure on my hands."

"Getting married adventurous?" Nick looked as if he didn't believe it. Uncle Ludovic smiled.

"But I'm sure we can make it an adventure with a happy end," he said. "And now let's finish this canoe."

10. A Pirate Reformed

On the morning of his wedding day, Uncle Ludovic, boatbuilder and part-time pirate, had an unexpected surprise. He woke up to find Nicholas standing beside him with a cup of tea.

"Goodness me," said Uncle Ludovic. "It's years since anyone brought me a cup of tea in bed. It makes it seem all worthwhile — getting married I mean."

"I thought we'd get up now and get ready before Mum and Dad come from the hotel," Nick replied. "After all, it's our wedding and not theirs."

"My own feelings precisely," Uncle Ludovic agreed. "We don't need people in smart Australian clothes to tell us how to run our weddings do we?"

"I was glad to see them," Nick added anxiously, in case Uncle Ludovic misunderstood him. "It's just that . . . " and his words ran out. By now he felt that

Caroline and he had invented Uncle Ludovic, and should be the ones to see Rosie and Ludovic properly married without any bossing from anyone else.

Not many wedding days start with a swim before breakfast, but Uncle Ludovic's did. Caroline, Nick, Uncle Ludovic and Rosie came down to the beach with their towels and plates of breakfast just as they had come so often in the past. There was another person who came down for the wedding-morning swim too — someone who knew the beach well. Rosie's tall tawny daughter Alison had come home to be a bridesmaid with Caroline. Together they swam and splashed and laughed and then sat in the special early sunshine eating and listening to the rustle and sigh of the waves on the sand.

"It seems like the first day of the holiday — not the last," Caroline said with something of a sigh herself. "It seems like the beginning and not the end."

"It isn't really an end," Rosie told her gently. "Good times don't end as easily as all that. We've just got to get on to the next thing — that's all. So Caroline, you'd better come home with Alison and me. You'll have to have a shower to get the salt off you for one thing. I want sweet bridesmaids, not salt ones."

Uncle Ludovic and Nick climed the hill track alone. "First there was just us," Nick said with a sigh, "and then everyone in the world came visiting . . ." It seemed a hundred years since Uncle Ludovic had pushed David Carter out of his canoe into the warm clear water of the bay.

"We're people of the world ourselves," said Uncle

114

Ludovic. "If we don't let the world visit us, we get lonely sooner or later."

Bunty bleated and stamped her feet in the purple and white foam of the alyssum border. Nick's mother and father stood by the open door looking gingerly into the empty house, like mice looking into a mouse trap.

"Here we are!" Nick called.

"For goodness sake," his mother replied, "look at you both! I'm glad Rosie didn't see you looking so damp and sandy on your wedding day Ludovic. She'd have called the whole thing off at once."

Neither Nick nor Uncle Ludovic told Mrs Gillian Battle that they had just left Rosie looking rather damp and sandy herself. They marched meekly inside looking at each other sideways. Gillian Battle kissed them both briskly.

"You really need me to look after you," she said contentedly, "and to get you to the church on time."

"Actually," Uncle Ludovic replied in a small voice, "I haven't had time to discuss this, you only arriving yesterday and all, but we're not getting married *in* the church ——"

"There!" Gillian Battle interrupted him. She looked at her husband Andy Battle sternly as if something was his fault. "I told you — I said to you when I first heard that, if there was a way of ruining a wedding, your brother Ludovic would find it some-how."

"I'm not ruining any wedding," cried Uncle Ludovic indignantly. "It's just that I've got a fancy to be married in my own garden."

"Your garden!" exclaimed Mrs Battle. "You can't call a bit of grass and a few trees a garden. And what about that sheep?"

"Bunty?" Uncle Ludovic said. "I don't see any difficulty. She could be a sort of woolly bridesmaid."

"A bride's sheep!" suggested Nick, "with flowers in her wool!"

"Well, I wash my hands of you both," Mrs Battle shrugged and laughed, but she didn't wash her hands of them after all. Instead she whisked Nick away, and started cleaning him up, helping him to put on his best clothes and brushing his hair so hard she seemed to suspect it of secret wickedness.

In the next room Andy Battle did the same for Uncle Ludovic. Nick could hear them laughing. Their voices, whether talking or laughing, sounded very much the same. Without the faces to watch, it was hard to tell which voice belonged to who.

"Oh dear!" said Mrs Battle rather sadly. "Your father's so pleased to be back here. He used to live in this little cottage you know and he loves the whole place. We had a marvellous time in Aussie, but I'm sure he's enjoying this bay more than the whole Gold Coast."

"Of course," said Nick. "It's a special place to be. I love it more than anywhere — except home, that is. Home's the best."

Mrs Battle looked more cheerful and gave him a hug so he smelt her rich expensive smell — a smell of clean new clothes and flowery scent.

"You can love any place you please," she said, "as long as you like home best."

"Come on, Sunshine!" yelled Andy Battle. "Let that boy alone! We're ready and I'm sure he is too."

Mrs Battle was amazed at the sight of Uncle Ludovic in his new suit and polished shoes. She walked around him, looking at him from all angles.

"Good heavens Gilly — you look as if you're thinking of buying him," Andy Battle said.

"He's already taken," Nick added.

"Oh, pooh to that!" said Mrs Battle lightly. "If he stays like that for ten minutes I'll fall over with shock. I want something a bit more stable." And she slipped her hand happily through Andy's arm.

Soon after this, wedding guests began to arrive. Murray Morgan arrived and so did the Morpeths, but without the Morpeth baby, who was too young to enjoy a good wedding. Other neighbours came carrying flowers and unexpected wedding presents. One man brought a new sort of glue, supposed to be particularly good for boatbuilding, one woman brought a basket of fern roots which she said she would plant in a cool place in Rosie's own bit of native bush. All the presents were rather strange and many of them were useful too. The guests carried chairs outside and Murray and Jeff produced a settee from the back of Jeff's van. The garden began to look as if something unusual was going to happen in it. When Rosie and her bridesmaids, with Mrs Russell and Mrs Russell's sister came down the track between the two houses there was somewhere for them to sit comfortably among the pools of light under the leaves.

"Honestly," Nick heard Mrs Russell say, "it's

hard to look on this as a wedding at all. It's more of a picnic."

He longed to stick up for Uncle Ludovic — to tell Mrs Russell that your own garden full of trees and flowers you had planted yourself was a good place to get married in, but to his surprise his mother said it all for him. Looking extremely smart in her Australian clothes Gillian Battle replied,

"Oh well, it wouldn't suit me but somehow it seems very right for Ludovic and Rosie. A church wedding is lovely of course, but this place is special to Ludovic, and it must be nice to get married in a place where every little thing means something to you. And Rosie's dress is just beautiful."

Nick thought Rosie did look beautiful. He was used to seeing her in blue, but today she wore a long golden dress, and had her hair done up high with a Spanish comb at the back of it. Alison and Caroline wore dresses of the same material with frills at the hemline and yellow daisies in their shining hair. Although these were not outdoor clothes they did not look out of place in Uncle Ludovic's funny little garden, for the sun sent arrows of golden light down through the leaves of the tree and Rosie, Alison and Caroline matched the sunlight well.

David Carter, wearing proper minister's clothes, suddenly appeared down the track from the garage.

"No pirate behaviour," Caroline said sternly to Uncle Ludovic.

"Oh no," said Uncle Ludovic meekly. "Pirate behaviour will be as far from my thoughts as tattooed mermaids."

The actual wedding ceremony was very short. Nick passed the ring at the right moment and Uncle Ludovic and Rosie were actually married, The register was signed in Uncle Ludovic's sitting-room, that very room with walls like honey and the trapdoor in the ceiling. There was a lot of hugging. Uncle Ludovic actually hugged Mrs Russell very boldly and looked so happy that she was surprised into giving him a real smile and hugging him back.

When Nick had been old enough to understand about telegraph lines, he had been fascinated from time to time to think that, over his head, people were talking, telling good news and bad news, laughing, crying, talking about babies, deaths, the high price of eggs and a thousand other things, both important and unimportant. Now he got the same feeling as the grown-up voices talked over his head about weddings in the past and possible weddings to come. Caroline nudged him.

"Pirate and wife," she said, and laughed. "It all ends happily."

"Yes, but our holidays are over too," Nick replied. "Just as I get used to things they're over."

"Well, we might come again," Caroline suggested hopefully.

"There won't be another holiday like this one." Nick shook his head. No next time would ever be so unexpected and mysterious.

"I thought Uncle Ludovic's wedding might be a bit more surprising," Caroline went on in a complaining voice. "It was very ordinary really."

"Lots of things can happen yet," said Rosie's

Alison, listening and looking amused.

Nick had known that Uncle Ludovic would not interrupt his wedding with any pirate game. All the same he knew what Caroline meant. It was as if Uncle Ludovic was changing before their very eyes into an ordinary uncle with a wife and even a family if you counted Alison — none of the unexpected side of him, the pirate side as Nick still thought of it, seemed to be left at all. Like Caroline, Nick found he was watching for the pirate to appear occasionally, and missing him when he did not reveal himself. Nick knew too that, even when he and Caroline went home again, things would never be quite the same as they had been, for now they understood new things about each other and about themselves. Caroline, for example, had stepped into Uncle Ludovic's pirate story because there was a place for her in it, because she liked to play a part. She could be a pirate or a pirate-reformer. It all depended upon what life offered her. He, Nicholas, would never forget that beyond the streets and the warm glow of the street lights was the sand and the sea and Antofagasta, a city on the other side of the world with street lights of its own.

Lunch at Rosie's was a very cheerful meal with turkey and champagne. Mrs Russell smiled at Uncle Ludovic more and more showing clearly that he had at last been accepted by the good society he had *said* he wanted to belong to.

Nick should have felt pleased but instead he felt, unexpectedly, something close to sadness. Was Uncle Ludovic really being carried farther away all the time? Was he being reformed, not so much of piracy, but of adventure, of difference?

"Well," said Uncle Ludovic at last, "maybe we can leave you people to eat up the scraps. Rosie and I have to be off. We'll just change into something suitable and then we'll be away with a hiss and roar. Make sure you finish the champagne."

"And do the dishes," said Caroline in a reproachful voice. Uncle Ludovic laughed.

"A pirate is let off the dishes when he marries," he said; "it's one of the pirate rules."

Caroline brightened up at hearing the pirate rules referred to in this promising way.

"Did you manage to decorate the car?" Mrs Battle asked Andy, when Uncle Ludovic and Rosie had left the room.

"Yes, Murray and I have done a pretty thorough job on it," Andy Battle replied. "We've filled the glove box with confetti and tied several tins at the back, and done a few other things. Old Ludovic is getting the traditional send off where that's concerned anyway."

"I wonder what Rosie's going-away dress will be like," Mrs Battle went on dreamily. "I'll never forget my going-away dress. I wore it for years afterwards."

"Rosie hasn't said anything to me about her going-away dress," Mrs Russell said. "She's very independent you know. And original too. I'm sure her going-away frock will be something different."

Rosie's going-away clothes were different all right, but not in the way Mrs Russell approved of. Rosie and Uncle Ludovic appeared wearing blue jeans.

Rosie wor.e a blue shirt and Uncle Ludovic wore a red one. Mrs Russell gave a cry of dismay. "Oh no, Rosie! And you always look so lovely when you're nicely dressed too!"

"That's as maybe," said Rosie firmly, "but a nice dress wouldn't suit the big *Sinbad* at all."

Nick's heart leaped. "You're going to go to sea after all — go sailing away in the big *Sinbad*," he cried.

"Yes!" said Uncle Ludovic. "Those wishing to wave goodbye to us will have to walk down onto the beach. We're setting off that-a-way," and he pointed out to sea.

"Oh strike!" Andy Battle said in disgust. "To think Murray and I went to a lot of trouble decorating your car for you. I just didn't give *Sinbad* a thought."

"Well, I think it's lovely," said Alison a little fiercely. "And when I get married I'm going to marry a sailor and set off to sea just like Ludovic and Rosie."

Then everyone began to talk at once. Uncle Ludovic and Rosie had their things packed in long canvas bags with draw strings at the top. They picked these up where they had hidden them and then everyone set off down the path from Rosie's place onto the beach. The early morning shine was gone. The surface of the sea was rippled with wind.

"I'd forgotten it was so quiet," Nick heard his father say. "There's not a breaker in here behind the rocks. It's incredible, really."

"Oh, breakers do get in," Uncle Ludovic said. "A sou-westerly wind and a high tide bring them in — don't you remember the storms?"

122

Nick thought he would like to be there during a storm . . . to help get the boats secured and hear the boom of the breakers on the beach. There was still more to find out about the bay and probably about Uncle Ludovic too.

"I'd forgotten the storms," Andy Battle replied. "When I look back it seems as if the sun shone all the time. And those pirate stories you told me about your wicked past were all told on sunny days. Oh well — you've reformed now."

"I wouldn't be too sure of that," said Rosie darkly.

On the jetty Uncle Ludovic turned.

"We thank you all," he said, "for helping us celebrate our wedding. And now, though we're going to be away for a week or ten days, we don't want to feel that the celebrations are going to stop." He passed something over to Andy Battle. "There are the keys to my cottage," he said. "Rosie and I will live in her house when we come back. She and Alison have too many possessions to fit comfortably into mine. But my cottage will be free now for friends and relations to use in the weekends and holidays, and I'd like them to begin using it as soon as possible. There are boats in the big shed in the next bay, the canoe is painted, and there is a cherry cake in the tin. There's no reason why you shouldn't all be here to welcome us back."

"Oh Daddy — can we stay?" Caroline cried. "You haven't seen me take my toe off the bottom and swim."

"Let's stay," Nick cried at the same moment.

"Well, I've got until the end of the week anyway,"

Andy Battle said. "If your mother is agreeable we could stay on a bit."

"Please! Please!" Nick and Caroline cried to their mother while Rosie and Uncle Ludovic swung neatly into big *Sinbad*.

"Oh, for goodness sake . . . three against one," Mrs Battle cried. "Oh, all right then; all right then!"

"That's the girl, Gilly," Uncle Ludovic said.

"I knew you'd win in the end," Mrs Battle called; "you never give up, do you?"

"Look, Gilly," Uncle Ludovic said, "Andy doesn't want to live here for good does he? And even if he did there isn't any room for him now is there?"

With Rosie in the wheel house big *Sinbad* began to move, little *Sinbad* bobbing behind. The engine thudded away echoing in the hills of the headland. Rosie smiled and shouted, "Goodbye! Goodbye!"

Uncle Ludovic appeared again wiping his hands on an oily rag and joined in the waving.

"Goodbye! Goodbye."

The water danced and swelled, spangled with light, a sea breeze stirred the fine wedding clothes, a seagull gave its curious lonely cry and somewhere on the beach Bunty bleated, staring across the bay towards the jetty.

Nicholas looked secretly at Caroline. She had a busy bright-eyed look on her face.

"It's important to make our plans now," she said, "because being married hasn't really changed him has it? He's gone all piraty again and anything — anything — could happen when he comes back."